Fair-Skinned Brunette

with the

Porcelain Shine

A Novel

John Bare

John Bare 11/4/21

Fair-Skinned Brunette with the Porcelain Shine

The opinions expressed by the author are not necessarily those of
Wisdom House Books, Inc.

Published by Wisdom House Books, Inc.
Chapel Hill, North Carolina 27516 USA
1.919.883.4669 | www.wisdomhousebooks.com

Wisdom House Books is committed to excellence in the publishing industry.

Book design copyright © 2021 by Wisdom House Books, Inc. All rights reserved.

Cover and Interior Design by Ted Ruybal

Published in the United States of America

Paperback ISBN: 978-1-7349884-0-6
LCCN: 2020921017

FIC022000 | FICTION / Mystery & Detective / General
FIC022100 | FICTION / Mystery & Detective / Amateur Sleuth
FIC027110 | FICTION / Romance / Suspense

First Edition

25 24 23 22 21 20 / 10 9 8 7 6 5 4 3 2 1

Table of Contents

Acknowledgments vii

Chapter 1 1

Chapter 2 7

Chapter 3 13

Chapter 4 19

Chapter 5 25

Chapter 6 31

Chapter 7 37

Chapter 8 43

Chapter 9 49

Chapter 10. 55

Chapter 11. 61

Chapter 12. 67

Chapter 13. 71

Chapter 14. 75

Chapter 15. 79

Chapter 16. 83

Chapter 17. 87

Chapter 18. 93

Chapter 19. 97

Chapter 20. 101

Chapter 21. 107

Chapter 22. 111

Chapter 23. 117

Chapter 24. 123

Chapter 25. 129

Chapter 26. 133

Chapter 27. 139

Chapter 28. 145

Chapter 29. 149

Chapter 30. 153

Chapter 31. 159

Chapter 32. 163

Chapter 33. 169

Chapter 34. 175

Chapter 35. 179

Chapter 36. 183

Chapter 37. 187

Chapter 38. 189

Chapter 39. 193

Chapter 40. 197

Chapter 41. 203

Chapter 42. 207

Chapter 43. 211

Chapter 44. 215

Chapter 45. 219

Chapter 46. 223

Chapter 47. 227

Chapter 48. 231

Chapter 49. 237

Chapter 50. 243

Chapter 51. 247

Chapter 52. 249

Chapter 53. 253

Chapter 54. 259

Epilogue 263

About the Author 287

Acknowledgments

You wouldn't be reading this book but for Betsy, my wife of twenty-eight years, who passed away in September 2020 from COVID-19. Betsy cheered on everyone she knew. For me and so many others she touched, Betsy made us believe we were as gifted as she imagined. Betsy's unrestrained pursuit of things that brought her joy inspired me to chase novels, songwriting, and photography. Whatever you like about the book, it's thanks to Betsy. Visit BetsyRossBare.com to learn more about Betsy and the amazing life she led.

The notion of a character named Lassie James flickered to life in the mid-1980s in apartment Z-4, in the Old Well complex in Carrboro, NC. As I aged, so did Lassie. Along the way, old Chapel Hill friends Steve Ferguson, Jeff Cobb, Clint Burgess, Denise Flett, Beth Rosenkampff, and Lynne Mohr nudged me keep the project alive. In the last couple of years, I put the first Lassie James story on paper. Thanks to Penny McPhee, Alice Rolls and Jill Vialet for providing feedback through the drafts.

By pure luck and good fortune, recording artist and producer Don Dixon brought the Lassie James lyrics to life. Together we created twelve original songs that accompany the book. You can access the album, *Lassie James Songbook Vol. I*, on music streaming services. Don played bass and assembled an all-star band for the recording sessions, with Jim Brock on drums, Beth McKee on piano and accordion, Matt Smith on pedal steel and dobro, Robert Kirkland on acoustic guitar, Mitch Easter on electric guitar, and Jeffrey Dean Foster on vocals. We recorded everything at Mitch's Fidelitorium studio in Kernersville. Tammy White assisted with production. Laura Pritchard-Compton designed the album cover art. Thanks to Chris Stamey's talent and skill, we could integrate the sheet music for Fair-Skinned Brunette into the book's cover design.

At Wisdom House, Ted, Clara, and Lauren took a pile of pages and made it a book. I'm grateful for their skill and precision.

Chapter 1

There is a fair-skinned brunette, she plants in the spring.
She wears a big hat, to keep her cheeks soft.

Her shoulders get red, in the Halifax sun.
She appears in my dreams, when angels carry me off.

She hangs jeans on her hips.
And sheets on the line.
The fair-skinned brunette.
With the porcelain shine.

*M*onday night in October. Sitting at the bar at Pig Farm Tavern in Chapel Hill. 11:57 p.m.

Fats just walked into the bar.

I can smell the lavender in her hair. Most of all, I feel the crackle, as if her skin is spitting electric charges into the air. She walks into a room, and everything goes static. Even with my back to the place, I know she's here.

I had been in deep conversation with the bartender, Siler, who is also the tavern owner and a very old friend. We were debating biscuits and gravy. These nouvelle cuisine chefs just don't get the pepper seasoning right.

Now Siler is looking past me. Red flush runs up his neck, through his cheeks and into his temples. He picks up my glass of Bulleit Rye and finishes it.

I hear Fats racking up the pool table, rolling the nine-ball set back and forth over the felt.

"Siler," she calls out, as casual as if she'd never left. "Pour me one of those."

The *crack* of the break.

"In fact," she goes on, "pour one for yourself. And a fresh one for Lassie. On me."

There's not another soul in the place.

Her cue pops again, and balls scramble around the table.

I am Lassie. My birth certificate, signed by a New Orleans doctor a half-century ago, reads Lassiter James Battle. Students at my high school in Saluda, on the edge of the Nantahala National Forest, knew me as James Battle. Later, that became my byline at the *Post*.

Fats, Siler, and a handful of old friends from Chapel Hill dubbed me Lassie James. These were the folks who rode out the blistering heat of freshmen orientation week, which unfolded without air conditioning or inhibition.

Feels like that was a hundred years ago.

I guess it was closer to thirty. Or thirty-two? Useless to work out the math. We've all lost the energy for precision, at this point. All that matters now is that we're all rolling up on age fifty, closer to death than to freshman year.

Last time I saw Fats, she was naked as a baby. We had just graduated from the University of North Carolina. We were scheduled to leave Chapel Hill that day to elope, ready to drive to Vegas to start the rest of our lives as husband and wife.

In hindsight, I can tell you we were both hungover that morning. At the time, I didn't know what a hangover was. Every morning felt that way, the only way.

We fell asleep after making love on the floor of apartment number Z-4 in the Old Well complex. Fell asleep right there on the shag carpet, tangled up in legs, wetness and a cotton quilt.

When the sunrise brought us into consciousness, Fats stood up, reached her hands toward the ceiling to stretch out the cramped muscles.

"My wedding-day gift to you: I'm going to get biscuits," she said.

Not a stitch of clothing on her. Long dark hair, light fair skin. Her nipples soft. Her ribs poking out. Eyes the color of brass cymbals. Six freckles running down her left shoulder, as if stars of a general. Bright red lips, wet like cranberry sauce, against her pale skin. Her lips looked painted on.

And on that long-ago morning, I watched her walk over to the sofa to grab her jeans. Her skin seemed lit from underneath, some sheath of white light draped over her muscle and bone, and her skin fitted over the illumination. I heard the door close and her car start. She was headed to Sunrise Biscuit Kitchen, a source of something both nutritional and medicinal. A bacon-egg-and-cheese biscuit and cinnamon roll were the only things that could sop up the booze still percolating through us.

I never saw her again. At least not in person. When Time magazine put Fats on the cover, claiming her medical research promised to save America, I saw her then. Plenty of times, I saw her on TV. Then, I saw her on red carpets with celebrity business partners.

She never came back to Z-4 that morning.

Three days later, I received a package in the mail.

Inside was a bacon-egg-and-cheese biscuit and a cinnamon roll. Stale, banged up, and beyond the sell-by date. But edible. So, I sat alone in Z-4 and ate the days-old meal and stared at her note.

"I can get you the biscuit. I can't marry you. I miss you, but I need to make a new adventure. On my own, for now. Let's take the summer. Then meet up in the fall and watch the leaves change."

—I love you, Fats.

That was the note. I threw it into the lake. We never met up. We never again watched the leaves change.

Fats was always the smart one.

I was crazy enough that I really would have eloped. She figured out we had been living in a bubble of undergraduate exuberance, delusion, and indulgence. All of which was magical but none of which indicated we should or could build a life together.

So, she ran away from me. And she made a life better than I could have given her.

I had probably done better, also—that is, better than I would have with her. I bopped around the globe on reporting assignments, without ever worrying about a trailing spouse, and ended up with a

Pulitzer citation on my wall. When the journalism business shrank, I moved on to free-lance writing and relocated back here in Chapel Hill to take a PhD in sociology.

So, no hard feelings, right?

The taste of stale biscuit rose in my throat.

Now, she's in Pig Farm with me, ten feet behind me. Working the pool stick around the table and buying me rye whiskey.

Siler poured his. Poured mine. He came around from behind the bar and walked over to the pool table and set her glass down on a high-top table cluttered with chalk and postcards promoting live music shows.

I didn't turn around. I could hear them speaking. Pausing to hug. Heard their glasses clink. Heard Fats be profane and Siler laugh loud enough to cover the music.

My iPhone was sitting on the bar. I punched up the TouchTunes app that let me control the jukebox remotely.

Alejandro Escovedo's voice boomed through the speakers. How he likes her better when she walks away.

"Lassie," I heard her call out.

She waited. I drank my rye. I didn't turn around. I didn't speak.

Fats yelled: "Wanna hang out 'til sunup and watch the leaves change?"

Fats. Forever the pool hustler.

Chapter 2

There is a fair-skinned brunette who curses in French.
She winked at me once, from an old white Corvette.

I showed her the stars, and she cried at Orion.
We poured Lagavulin and sang Tammy Wynette.

She hangs jeans on her hips.
and sheets on the line.
The fair-skinned brunette.
with the porcelain shine.

*E*scovedo's song stopped. Pig Farm was quiet.

Siler was back around the bar. He took up his usual spot, leaning on his right elbow. Drink in his left hand. Dumb look on his face. He believed patrons drank more from a bartender who was nonjudgmental. Siler was the smartest dumb-looking guy I had ever seen.

Fats took up the stool beside me.

Clinked her glass into mine. She drank. I drank. Siler drank.

We all sat there and let the rye do the talking.

After thirty years, the extended silence seemed appropriate. The silence was more comfortable than conversation. One long moment, making the transition from then to now, from young to old, from old to new, from bulletproof to fragile, from looking out dreamily toward life's horizon to walking up to the edge of its cliff.

"Thanks for the biscuit," I said, finally turning toward her and catching my breath at the way she had aged into a captivating beauty. Fats was shimmering. Still.

"Play me one of yours," she said, nodding toward the iPhone on the bar.

In the old days, I had been writing songs with several local bands. She always liked the secret knowledge of a lyric she had inspired.

I had kept at it over the years. For a long time, it was like I was playing a joke on myself. Kept writing songs on the side, but no one in the music business showed interest.

Then, in the last ten years or so, I started to find some songwriting partners. I was beyond thrilled. Through the various collaborations, I had co-written a dozen songs that made the final cut of albums. But the agate print of songwriting credits is pretty abstruse stuff. Surprised Fats knew.

Siler was aware I was writing some songs, but I don't think he could tell you much about which tunes were mine and which weren't. Mostly, he liked the road trips to Nashville.

My song writing credits were under the name they both knew: Lassie James.

I worked the app and dialed up a Jeffrey Dean Foster tune I had co-written, "Brownsville Tonight."

Buenos dias, mi amigo, have you seen my friend?
Have you seen the pretty girl who taught me how to sin?

Mexican topaz, she shimmers at night.
Her skin is electric and gives off white light.

How many stars in Boca del Rio? How many stars in old New Orleans?
How many stars in Nuevo Laredo? How many stars in Sweetwater Springs?

How many stars can fit in the sky?
How many stars in Brownsville tonight?
How many stars in Brownsville tonight?

"Congratulations," Siler said, looking at Fats. "The ceremony tomorrow?"

"It's Thursday," she said. "Big la-di-da at McCorkle Place. Academic gowns, bunting, and the works. Mostly an excuse to get back here. I've been away a long time."

Every October 12th, the University celebrates the anniversary of the laying of the cornerstone of Old East Dorm, the oldest building at the oldest state university in the country. On the day of the annual celebrations, the University also presents awards to distinguished graduates.

This year, Fats would be among the alums up on stage being recognized.

Chancellor Sanders Mallette, who had been one of the great journalism professors before taking the administrative role, would be presenting the honor to Fats. The event would double as Mallette's inauguration. He'd been named chancellor a couple of months back, put in place to clean up the world-class academic fraud scandal driven by an athletic department that had become a professional subsidiary of the university.

I had known Mallette since my sophomore year, when I was in his intro newswriting class. Then he had served as my doctoral adviser for the past three years, and he was still chairing my dissertation committee. I was scheduled to defend the dissertation next week. Assuming a successful defense on Monday, I would be in position to secure a PhD.

In between the old undergraduate days and returning to campus for grad school, Mallette became a friend and mentor, and something more. When I was on top—when I received the Pulitzer, when my name was above the fold in papers across Europe—I would get a call from Mallette. Always with gentle reminders to focus on service to others, ways I could give back.

Whenever things turned sour—when my fiancé ditched me in London, when the shrinking industry sent me packing—he would always call with a boost. A new lead, a new opportunity. Somehow he knew. The man was blessed with timing.

When the *Post* offered another round of buyouts, another step toward self-immolation, Mallette called again, even before the news hit the wire. He knew. He always knew.

"We've got a spot for you here in Chapel Hill," he said. "Come do the PhD program, and then join us on faculty."

"You can teach and do free-lance writing gigs," he said. "And you'll have more time to write those hit songs. You'll be a man of letters, like Kristofferson."

Still waiting on the hit song. Otherwise, his forecast was true. With the buyout, the free-lance writing income, and the surprise of modest songwriting royalties, I could afford a few luxuries. And a PhD was a luxury. I never expected to teach sociology—or anything else. But I could check it off the bucket list.

Fats reached over and squeezed my hand.

"I love 'Brownsville Tonight,'" she said. "I played it for the Texas governor from my phone on my last trip to Austin. The electric guitar is incredible."

Siler kept his dumb look. Bartenders don't care about name dropping.

"But I was thinking of another one," she said. "You know I always got weak in the knees when you wrote a line about me."

I finished my rye. The bottle of Bulleit was draining. The whiskey was down below the bottle's green label. Siler poured me more. Put a fresh bottle on the bar as backup, the way a gunnery sergeant might set a spare magazine nearby when he senses the machine gun running low.

"You know the one," she said, leaning her body sideways and bumping her shoulder into mine.

"There I am at the White House for a celebration of the American arts, and I have to hear it from some Smithsonian honoree. A woman needs to hear about that kind of song from the source."

Siler looked like he might doze off.

I knew the song.

She knew me, still. How to get inside my head.

My fingers worked the app.

Jeffrey Dean Foster's voice filled the jukebox speakers, singing about the "Fair-Skinned Brunette with the Porcelain Shine."

My back shivered as Jeffrey Dean sang the lyrics I had imagined and written about the sexiest girl I knew so long ago. I felt the hum of her heartbeat even from a distance, and knew art was imitating life imitating art again.

"Welcome home," I said, turning back her way and this time holding her eyes with mine. "I'd love to watch the leaves change with you."

Fats reached for the bottle and emptied the rye into her glass.

"What are we gonna do 'til sunup?" she asked.

Siler yawned.

Chapter 3

She wears two shades of lipstick and never waits in line.
She carries mini-bottles, and a knife to cut up limes.

She's the Queen of Whiskey Glam. Jack Daniel's meet Kate Spade.
She always wins at Twister. She played the Turf back in the day.

*T*he rest of the world knew Fats as Dr. Holly Pike, the face of a new generation of scientists ready to transform global health.

After Fats walked out of Z-4, she moved to New York and began taking graduate classes at Columbia. As she had been at UNC, she was a star there.

At Columbia, Fats ultimately took a PhD in chemistry and also a law degree. In her summer law firm work, she specialized in intellectual property.

My old girlfriend started figuring out how to design and program cells to behave differently. She took patents on every innovation.

The Big Pharma companies all wanted her, and the law firms were fighting to get her. Federal agencies and global NGOs that fund scientific research wanted her to set up a lab that would focus on breakthrough public-health research.

She set up a lab at Columbia and created a one-of-a-kind center of applied research, intellectual property, and public health.

At first, all of this made Fats a minor celebrity within a highly specialized, arcane field.

Then, she designed a drug to grow hair. She became as famous as a Kardashian.

It wasn't exactly a drug, she explained.

Siler queued up the jukebox with the late John Prine. Then Merle, George, Waylon, Kris, and more Merle. The live version of "Yesterday's Wine" always made Siler cry.

The FDA puts inventions into different categories.

First, there are devices; this includes everything from a Q-tip to a penile implant. Medical devices must be approved by the FDA, and the government tracks problems, recalls, and so on. Huge business.

Second, there are drugs. Crestor, for example, is one of the big-time drugs docs prescribe for folks who need assistance in lowering cholesterol levels. Another huge business.

Third, there are biologics; this is a kind of medicine built from living cells or a biological source—not man-made chemicals. Humira, the arthritis medicine advertised on TV, is a biologic. Vaccines and gene therapy are examples of biologics. Over the next generation, this will become bigger business than devices and drugs combined.

"When I was a doc student, we would hang out at a pub in New York and laugh about the riches coming to the first person to find a cure for male-pattern baldness," Fats said.

"Given that erectile dysfunction drugs are all over the market, a cure for baldness was the last cash cow out there for quality-of-life drugs. It seemed like a lark at the time. Then, when I started the lab, I was grinding away on solutions for diseases in developing countries and seeking funding for cancer research and more. We have this incredible untapped potential to improve health—if we just had the funding. Up late one night, it hit me: Stop applying for funding and generate my own. So, I pulled together a team and spent a year figuring out male-pattern baldness."

Once through the clinical trials, FDA red tape, and so on, Fats was printing money. She owned the intellectual property and the rights to the science and was the sexy face of a cure millions of men wanted—and millions of women wanted for men.

From our UNC connections, Fats linked up with some rising stars in professional basketball and football to serve as the first pitchmen. They created a Jennie-Craig-style before-and-after campaign.

Wheres a previous generation of stars made bald beautiful, these young sports celebrities emerged in the "after" TV commercials with heads of hair that could have landed them on *The Mod Squad*.

The treatment—a biologic—was marketed as NextGen Hair, through a new company that a couple of the pro athletes and Fats launched together.

On the day of the IPO, she became a billionaire, for the first time.

"I went from a prestigious, but little-known, research lab to TMZ cameras following me around with my team of All-Stars," she laughed. "Columbia didn't know what to do."

Through a series of trusts, private firms, and publicly-traded companies, Fats organized a wealth-management strategy to fund a combination of public-health research and highly profitable designer medicines. Through what Time magazine called a virtuous spiral, Fats was making money faster than she could spend it—in the literal sense.

Money from putting hair on heads and other designer treatments was funding work that would rein in Ebola and was showing promising signs with cystic fibrosis and uterine cancer – and now rapidly being applied to the rise of new Coronaviruses.

"It was like we kept having hit records. One biologic would hit, then another, then another. I started living well, even with whole streams of revenue carved off to fund my lab and the trusts. Crazy as it sounds, I outgrew Columbia."

Fats described how she created a corporation with a sister organization—a foundation—with labs in Tokyo, Budapest, Lima, Cape Town, New York, and Atlanta. Her ventures became so profitable, she invited three rounds of debt and equity funding. She was over-subscribed each time.

Forbes doesn't know where to put her on the list, but she's in the top 400. And expected to be the top woman on the list next year.

Siler was wearing a ball cap with the logo from Goody's headache powder. He lifted it and winked at Fats. He had a good half-inch of hair on the top of his head, bristly from a brush cut.

"And I thank you," Siler said.

We were well into the second bottle of Bulleit.

A Tammy Wynette tune rolled up on the jukebox. We both looked at Siler.

He shrugged.

"Guess we need to go check out Orion," she said.

Fats opened the door and stepped out onto the back deck. The fall night had turned cold in Chapel Hill. Sky was clear. She pointed to the North.

Fats was in a short sky-blue dress with tights underneath. Knee-high white boots. A leather jacket was on a hook by the pool table.

Her black hair hung past her shoulder blades. Until the wind blew it sideways.

"What do you have to eat around here these days?" she asked, putting the question to the heavens.

"Biscuits. I'll go get some biscuits," Siler said, heading down the back stairs to Time Out for a supply of chicken-and-cheese biscuits.

"Put on some hot water, too. I'd like to get some green tea going," she said.

Fats came in off the porch, closed the door, and picked up the pool cue. Her face was flushed from the wind, her eyes watery and sparkly. She leaned on the cue, using it as a cane to stabilize her from the whiskey, the cold and the memories.

"I have a job for you," she said.

Chapter 4

Too old to please the pretty girls, too young to take the needle.
I'm stacking time with Crestor, and a heart that's growing feeble.

Green tea and green label,
keep my mind alert, my liver stable.
Doing less than I am able.
I've become The Displaced Man.
I've become The Displaced Man.

We switched from rye to green tea. Organic tea, Genmaicha. A green tea blended with toasted brown rice.

"Listen," I said, "I can't quite describe what it's like to see you again—or see you in person. I can't turn on the TV these days without seeing you. I know the old days are long ago and far away, like the song says, and neither one of us wants to revisit who did what way back when. I've been blessed beyond my imagination—blessed more than anyone I know, other than you, to be honest. And it's like having lightning strike for you to walk in here tonight. I knew you would be in town, for University Day. But I didn't expect to see you. And I certainly didn't expect to be up drinking whiskey with you."

"Tea," she interrupted. "We're drinking tea."

"And to be eating biscuits with you again . . ." I said, the sentence trailing off.

I was drunk. I was rambling. I didn't have a point, and I couldn't talk my way toward one. So, I did what smart drunks do. I shut up. I drank tea.

Ray Wylie Hubbard came on the jukebox, then Hayes Carll and Shooter Jennings. Then, Patsy Cline.

"So . . ." I started in again. Goddammit, I was going to find a point to make. I'm not that smart a drunk, after all.

"So, welcome home. Glad to see you. Glad you're here, Tar Heel born and bred and all that. Glad we're drinking whiskey. Glad Siler is getting biscuits. But I have a job. Or I don't need a job. Or I don't need a job from you. Or I don't know why you need me to do a job. Or don't care."

A long pause. Siler came back in. Closed the door to the cold blast.

"Let's just eat the fucking biscuits," I said, as triumphantly as I could sound.

Fats chomped off big bites of gooey cheese, fried chicken, and warm biscuit.

"I have a job for you," she said again.

Before I could swallow and reply, Siler jumped in.

"Cool. What you need him to do?" he asked.

"It's an inside job," she began.

Fats explained that her company, which she had named Gimghoul Research Labs, was a kind of hybrid. It included some pharmacology labs, with many scholars leading basic research, and a network of centers that were unifying genetics and pharmacological research. There was a product innovation department figuring out how to translate the R&D into consumer products—both the designer products driving the profit and the products promising to improve the human condition.

While many of the phases of the work required proprietary research and trade secrets, there were also parts of the work that required transparency and full disclosure. GRL, as her firm was known, had built its own publishing unit to create, vet, and publish findings from its research efforts and the research run by others. There was special emphasis placed on publishing findings that built bridges from the basic research to the applied research. This created a public record of evidence that helped make the case for consumer products.

"It's all bigger than I can manage—or anyone could manage. It's what keeps me up at night," Fats said, starting in on her second biscuit.

Siler poured her more tea. He had one glass of whiskey and one cup of coffee, alternating sips from one to the other.

"Okay, you're running a multi-national corporation that's making you billions of dollars," I said. "Seems fair you'd have some headaches. Nothing I can do about that. If you don't want the nightmares, sell the business. I'm sure Dow or Pfizer or somebody would give you a few billion for it. You can buy another house in the islands."

"I've bought a house on Gimghoul Road," she said.

That threw me.

"I'm moving home," she said. "I told you we would meet up in the fall to watch the leaves change. Well. It's *this* fall. I'm not here for the week to get some kind of award on University Day. I'm back in Chapel Hill to see you.

"And I have a job for you," she repeated.

"Hey, take the job," Siler said, sipping the whiskey, then the coffee, then the whiskey again.

The rye was still escalating in my system. The genmaicha couldn't knock down the alcohol. Fats never needed sleep. She was flying. My brain was whirring. My eyes were tired, and I could see a headache just ahead. I was overmatched.

"What's the job?" I asked, surrendering.

"I know you won a Pulitzer for uncovering the LIBOR fraud that helped create the financial crisis," Fats continued.

She was referring to the conspiracy among financial institutions to cook the numbers on the London Interbank Offered Rate. The LIBOR lending rates set the number on what it costs banks to borrow money from other banks, covering ten currencies and more than a dozen periods of time for loans. This trickles down the entire global financial system. If you're a newlywed in Little Rock looking for a home mortgage loan, you ended up paying a higher rate than you needed to when banks cooked the LIBOR numbers. Same if you're running a French apparel company that needs to borrow money to expand factories. You ended up paying too much in interest.

"You have a talent for finding needles in haystacks," Fats said. "GRL is publishing haystacks of research studies. I've been getting anonymous emails claiming there's fraud in my publishing units. I don't know if this is sour grapes from someone who didn't become the star researcher they wanted to be. Or if it's legitimate. But I know who can find out. You can find out.

"I'll hire you to run an investigative journalism project—an independent project. No oversight from me. I will have no editorial input. No approval rights. You can publish anything, anywhere. You get full access to everything in my shop that is not protected as a trade secret."

Siler spoke first: "How much does the gig pay?"

"We'll start with a year-long contract for $5 million," Fats said. She moved from the biscuit to a cinnamon roll.

"He'll take it," Siler said, and the two of them shook hands.

Chapter 5

I dreamed of San Francisco but wound up in Millbrae.
I used to want a book deal, but now there's nothing left to say.

I've mostly made my peace, don't wonder too much why.
But I still dream of Gimghoul Road, and the Pilgrim's Progress makes me cry.

Green tea and green label,
keep my mind alert, my liver stable.
Doing less than I am able.
I've become The Displaced Man.
I've become The Displaced Man.

It was somewhere between 3:00 and 4:00 a.m.

Fats had a high-end Coulee waiting outside, the heater running. There was a driver. The Coulee was the latest, space-age luxury electric vehicle.

We both got in the backseat.

"Nice ride," I said.

"It's new," she said, without humor, focusing on her phone. "A car designed for a scientist. It promises to text me weekly data. I'll be able to track its operations the way Delta can with its jet planes. And I can use an app to turn on the car and heat up the seats before I walk out the door in the morning."

The Coulee was a like a magic carpet. No engine. No sound. Wheels turning at the direction of a computer chip, not a combustion engine. I was riding inside a PowerPoint presentation.

All through the ride, Fats was swiping and poking the phone, wide awake, answering emails from her employees around the world and exchanging texts with her friends from the *Today Show*. Al and Savannah are witty with the texts. Who knew?

The green tea was starting to give me a second wind, or a third. I had a 9:00 a.m. appointment with Mallette to discuss my upcoming dissertation defense—how to manage the stagecraft, the egos on the committee, and the methods discussion. No sign of trouble. Just the kind of statistical conversation that scholars pursue. For the work, I was using a kind of time-series analysis. I appreciated the chance to hear any questions that had come up, ahead of next week's defense. It was coming up on Monday. Given that we were in the pre-dawn hours of Tuesday, that meant my defense was less than a week away.

And now, I was apparently a millionaire, thanks to Siler's negotiating skills.

"You're dropping me off. Have the driver head down South Columbia to Westwood," I said, figuring I could grab a couple of hours of sleep, take a boiling shower, and get to my meeting without too much damage.

"We're headed to my new place," she said. "I've got a guest house out back. It's yours, for now."

Fats didn't frame this as an invitation. Sounded more like a directive.

This was the CEO side of her that I had read about but never seen in person. Dr. Holly Pike had turned into an executive. The spontaneous girlfriend I knew, Fats, lived on mostly in my imagination.

The driver turned down Gimghoul and pulled into the drive of a sprawling Queen Anne home that had been expanded over the years. There was indeed a guest house out back.

Fats locked up her phone and exited the car.

"Come inside with me. Want to show you some things," she said.

The driver opened my door for me. I got out and followed Fats through the stone pathway, past the dogwoods and laurels and red tips, up the porch, and through the double doors of heavy, dark wood.

The living room was lit up and humming. Two laptop computers were open and alive. The TV was on CNN and muted. A Tumi computer case was on the sofa.

An attendant came in with a tray. There was a pot of coffee. There was a teapot with genmaicha steeping. She poured a cup for Fats.

"Thank you," Fats said to her staff. "You can head home now. Appreciate you getting us settled."

The attendant went back through the kitchen. I heard a back door open and close. I saw Coulee lights come on in the driveway. The driver was ferrying the attendant home.

"The day shift will come at 6:00," Fats said, seeing me watch the car pull away and assuming I was wondering who would brew the next pot.

Fats and I were alone. For the first time in thirty years.

I sank into the sofa. Numb from booze and caffeine and the thought of hiring an accountant to figure out the taxes on $5 million.

"I'll have a contract sent over to you by noon and a first check of $1.25 million," Fats said. "Quarterly checks for the same amount will follow, until we wrap the year. You can quit, or I can fire you—with thirty days' notice required, either way. Everything you learn, everything you hear, everything you write—it's all yours, as I promised. The only thing off limits are the trade secrets that I'm bound by legal agreement to protect."

She handed me a leather folio.

"Take a look at that and then hand it back. When I get the signed contract back from you, I'm making those files and more—several boxes, actually—available to you in the guest house out back. It will be your office."

The folio was soft and buttery. Money may not be able to buy happiness, but it sure buys better leather.

Inside were five pieces of paper, each 8.5" x 11"—just like what you'd get out of the copier at Kinko's.

On each page was a printed copy of an email sent to Fats, alleging fraud. On each email, the sender's name showed up as "Bootstrap."

The emails were brief and accusatory, without offering details. But the tone was serious, and the sender's persistence added to the gravity. The sender claimed that many peer-reviewed articles from GRL were fraudulent, that findings were being tweaked to enhance the professional standing of the authors and to enable individual researchers to profit.

"Those are the five most recent. It started back in the summer. Came once a week, maybe twice. Lately, it's been heating up," Fats said.

Each email was time stamped at 4:17 a.m. There was an email a day, for the past five days.

A buzzing interrupted the silence.

Fats reached for her phone. I looked at my watch. 4:17 a.m.

"Bootstrap is on time, once again," Fats said.

She read the email silently. Then, out loud to me.

Shame on UNC and Sanders Mallette for honoring the founder of a company tolerating fraud. Let's see what SM has to say when I reveal the fraud to him.

Chapter 6

Sweet Carolina Sunshine,
touches gentle on your mind.
It's always home again, In Carolina.
Ghosts still touch the land,
they'll lead you by the hand.
You can go home again, In Carolina.

A generation after she promised, we watched the leaves turn.

We walked down by Hippol Castle. The morning fog and the wetness of sunrise put a matte finish on the leaves. Dogwoods and maples were smeared with color, set off against the evergreens that filled in the spaces overhead.

We looped off the castle property, down into Battle Park. We moved along the same trails used by Kemp Plummer Battle, who was president of the University nearly 150 years ago. I had searched my family tree for a connection to Kemp but never found one. Still, the park had always felt like my personal place.

Fats could have been sprinting the trails. The hills were getting to me this morning.

I had held my college weight, 180 pounds, and at six-feet tall, still presented an illusion of fitness. Yet somehow, the pounds were no longer distributed the way they had been back in college, and the lungs weren't as robust. I was chasing Fats and Father Time on that trail.

"So, what does 4:17 a.m. mean?" she asked.

"You tell me. You've got a global enterprise," I said. "That number could be tied to anything. Or it could be just a time zone thing. Say, Bootstrap is in London. Every morning at 9:17 UK time, he or she has a free moment to send you a note.

"Could be at precisely this moment every morning scary voices appear in his or her head and compel the action. Sometimes, crazy is just crazy. May be nothing rational or real about it all."

"Or," Fats picked up, "I could be getting scammed. Some disgruntled researcher could be cooking numbers and publishing the fraudulent work through GRL."

"No way to tell," I said, casually. I was more worried about the hills than the question.

"Yes, there is a way to tell. And you're going to find it. Because I'm paying you $5 million," Fats said, using her CEO voice.

"What if I solve this before the year runs out?" I asked, trying to poke at her a bit. "The deal Siler negotiated just gives me an incentive to collect the quarterly payments. If I solve it tomorrow, I'm leaving money on the table?"

"Okay, genius," she said, "you solve this in the first thirty days, and you get a $1 million bonus."

We were a few minutes away from the trail head at Park Place, where we would exit Battle Park for the residential street. This would leave us a good walk back to Gimghoul Road. I needed carbs more than I needed a longer walk.

The sunrise was burning off the morning haze. We covered the trail in silence. A couple of steps behind Fats, I was watching her ass toggle left and right like a metronome. She was in all black—black lululemon pants, black Patagonia jacket. Black gloves, black fleece hat. Black hair pulled back into a pony tail. Black Merrell boots. The white of her neck was visible above her collar. Just a few dots of sweat. Bright as a China serving dish.

Fats had stocked up the guest house for me with personal items – a wardrobe and a laptop loaded with GRL data and information. I was now a GRL contractor, so I had a GRL email address, password, and identity. She offered to have the company deliver boxes of hard copy files, but there was no need. Everything else was virtual. Beyond the work items, she had stocked the place with my genmaicha tea, protein bars, and all of the personal items that you'd find in a fancy hotel. She'd loaded in a bunch of trail shop clothing, so I was in a blue North Face jacket, gloves, and hat. Khakis from last night were taking a beating, and the lack of sleep was heightening my senses and dulling them at the same time. Then, she had included bowties, jackets, and slacks from Alexander Julian's store.

"How are your mom and dad?" she asked. Her first personal question. After all these years. After they thought Fats would be their daughter-in-law, a lifetime ago.

"Retired," I said. "Both in pretty good health."

"Did they ever move back to Saluda?" she asked.

Mom had been an English teacher, and Dad a math teacher when Fats knew them. Teaching middle school and high school in Hillsborough. Was surprised Fats remembered that they once had been so focused on retiring to a second home in Saluda, in the southwestern North Carolina mountains. I had forgotten that myself, until that moment. Reminded me how malleable our dreams really are.

"Not Saluda," I said. "In the Ukraine, in fact."

That stopped Fats for a moment. She turned and looked again, measuring my face to see if I was bullshitting. Raised her eyebrows.

"No lie," I continued. "In Kiev. They are missionaries for a progressive, faith-based organization. They're feeding hungry kids, saving orphaned girls from being sold into the sex trade."

"Damn," Fats said, and she was back to leading me through the trails.

"It's the real thing. Communication there is iffy. We try to check in around the first of each month. Sometimes, they can get a phone line out. Sometimes, not," I said.

"So, they traded Saluda for Kiev," Fats said.

"Now, there's a song lyric."

"Hey, send me a link to their group. I'd like to make a donation," she said.

"That would mean a lot to them. I will," I said.

Her ass kept toggling. Left. Then right. Then left. I was gonna be hypnotized.

I turned the conversation back to GRL.

"Who hates you?" I asked.

Fats turned her head and cut her eyes at me.

"Really. Who hates you? Someone is trying to do you harm—either through fraudulent research or by sending you harassing notes to cause you grief. So, who hates you?"

"'Hate' is a word for a freshman dorm," she said. "In my world, the only word is 'money.'"

"I have a lot of it. GRL makes lots of it. Nobody hates me. Nobody loves me. People just see a chance to make money through me—and through GRL. In most cases, this motivation is a good thing. Honest researchers know they can do good and do well at the same time. They can design a medical treatment that helps people enjoy their lives. Or they can find a cure for a disease that will extend lives in developing countries. And they make money along the way. My business depends on that. And ninety-nine percent of the time, it works."

She paused.

"Even when it doesn't work," she continued, "people want to keep open the chance to do business in the future. There's always another deal around the corner. So keep the relationship positive."

"Then what's new? Something has changed. There has been a trigger," I said.

"Lots of new things. The interesting new things are, for now, covered by that 'trade secrets' designation I mentioned," Fats said, turning back again to peek at me. "You're going to have to work for your million-dollar bonus."

"So how do I factor in 'trade secrets' when I'm solving this riddle?"

We were out of the trail and into the clearing by the lane.

"Watch the *Today Show* Wednesday morning," she said, this time without looking back.

Fats waved at a black car idling on the gravel. It pulled over. She opened the door and nodded for me to get in.

"The car will take you by your place. Pick up whatever you need and get settled in at Gimghoul. I need you in the guest house."

I slid over to make room for her. Fats chuckled and shook her head.

"The car is all yours. I'm going for a run now. I can't drag your ass around these trails all morning. Oh, and your 9:00 a.m. with Mallette has been moved to Gimghoul Road. He'll meet you in the guest house. I'm meeting with him at 11:00 to talk about a GRL partnership with the university."

She whipped the car door shut. She stretched down to touch her toes, then took off on a fast run, heading down South Boundary to Cameron Avenue. The black ponytail was bouncing.

"Where to?" the driver asked.

"Sunrise Biscuit Kitchen. God bless you," I said.

Chapter 7

Is today Monday, or could it be Sunday.
I really don't know how to find out.
Am I drunk now or sober? Is the week over?
The days and the nights are still jumbled about.
Maybe it's Sunday. It feels more like Monday.
Where's a newspaper with a date that will tell.

*T*uesday morning in October. Sitting at the bar at Pig Farm Tavern in Chapel Hill. 11:57 a.m.

Siler was in the position. Leaning his right elbow on the bar. Coffee in his left hand. Dumb look on his face. Carly Simon on the jukebox, the volume turned down to a whisper.

I was half-way through a takeout container of soup, split pea with ham. On my second heavy mug of genmaicha tea.

A scorching shower put some life back in me. Then, I wrapped the meeting with Mallette. We spent fifteen minutes discussing the defense, and more than an hour talking about life. It was always like that with Mallette.

"James," he said, "the doctoral defense is a custom, a ritual. We honor our history through these kinds of rituals. So on the one hand, it's busy work. The quality of your dissertation is unquestioned. On the other hand, it's a ritual that celebrates the commitment to creative contributions to a body of knowledge."

Mallette was flipping through my music CDs and pulled out a Hasil Adkins selection and put it in the spinner. The crazy West Virginian's voice peeled paint off the wall. Mallette lowered the volume.

"I've always believed the university should conduct doctoral defenses as public events," he continued. "We are the people's university. We should post bills across campus. Invite the public to fill the auditorium. To be part of our tribe as we honor years of work that add one more piece of knowledge to our collective understanding of the world, one more totem to our sacred bundle. Taken alone, any individual dissertation seems meaningless. Taken together, all the dissertations from a discipline cover a whole lot of what we know about the world."

"I'm good with a public event," I said. "The comprehensive exams were the tough spot. The dissertation defense should run fine."

A little Hasil goes a long way. Mallette kept flipping through the CDs while we talked. He swapped out Hasil for an Iris Dement CD. Hymns.

"I've Got That Old Time Religion," scorched through the speakers. Mallette raised the volume.

"Something I've never asked you," I said. "All those times. When I was sinking in London. When I was in trouble in St. Pete. How did you know to call? Your timing was spooky."

Iris kept singing. I refilled our mugs of hot tea.

"I'd love to tell you that I had some kind of line in to the angels," Mallette said. "I knew mountain women who had a kind of intuition that intrigued me. And frightened me. I used to dream that the mountains would make me a mystic."

"And they did?" I asked.

"No. The mountains filled me with empathy," he said. "Taught me how small we are in the world, and how big we can be in the moment. If we choose to be. If we look outside ourselves. I've spent my life trying to identify those moments. Those moments when I could do something big, when probably nobody else was going to do anything. It haunts us when we miss them."

Made sense. He always found moments when my life was suspended in mid-air. Moments when my stomach felt like it does when the roller coaster crests the very tip-top of the steepest rise, in the split second before gravity pulls everything down. When weightlessness made me feel sick and magical at the same time.

"However you did it," I said, "I'm grateful. Something more than grateful. It's difficult to express. I believe the mountains made you generous, also. A generous man in a world folding inward on itself, sucked into a black hole of tweets and selfies."

Mallette laughed. He hummed along with Iris. Lined up the edges of the row of CDs.

"Generous at moments, perhaps," he said. "More and more, I'm selfish with my time. It's like water running through my fingers. Time. I just need quiet moments, time. To read and think. I used to have hours. Now I steal away minutes."

He picked up his coat.

"Well, you found another moment," I said. "The University needs you in South Building, running things. We all need your time."

I shook his hand.

"The defense is a ritual," he repeated. He covered my hand in both of his. "Remember. We're like the third little pig. We build slowly. But with brick."

"I'll remember that," I said. "I'll look for moments to put all of this research to some good."

"Monday is a moment for you," Mallette said, "and you'll have plenty more moments to come. The trick is not to have them haunt you. To be big in the moment."

He walked over the stone path to the big house, to see Fats. The hymn from Iris matched his steps on the rocks.

Right then, nearly every cell in my body had wanted to nap. I overcame the urge and grabbed my backpack. Headed out across campus. Walked right into this barstool at Pig Farm. For soup. And tea. And Siler's conversation.

I didn't feel like a millionaire. But I felt something. Fats had left me a company iPhone. There were two numbers programmed in. One was her private cell. The other was the black car. I now had a driver. I now had two phones.

Siler was settling up winners and losers from his weekly NFL pool.

I met Siler when we were both eighteen years old. He was tall and skinny and carried a tennis racquet on campus and a joint behind his ear. He strutted into Chapel Hill from the far western mountains of North Carolina, a math major who got most of the answers right.

Tough thing is, most of the answers aren't good enough when you come down from the mountain.

By sophomore year, Siler was a music major. He carried a harmonica in his pocket and a guitar strapped over his shoulder. The tennis racquet was on the roof of Cobb Dorm, home to 363 girls. Siler had a thing for a girl living on the fourth floor of Cobb Dorm. In an instance lacking his usual genius, he was trying to get her attention late one night by tossing a pebble up to the window. When the pebble didn't reach that distance, he tried a tennis ball and then his tennis racquet. It landed on the roof and stuck. She never emerged at the window. He was a Romeo left wanting for his Juliet on the balcony.

Siler was pretty good at a lot of things.

He had found success as a roadie for various Texas musicians and troubadours. He became a master carpenter during a stay in New York, making fancy cabinets for rich folks. Now, besides Pig Farm, he has a small side business rebuilding engines for old BMWs. Very private–word-of-mouth referrals only. If he decided to take your case, Siler would rebuild the engine with the same care of a mama doting on a newborn.

Chapter 8

Yes, dear. Yes, dear.
I fixed the screen door, and I called the man.
I hooked up the Wi-Fi and rinsed off the pan.

Yes, dear. Yes, dear.
I bought a card for your mom and fixed the hinge on her gate.
Your hair looks good, and I see you've lost weight.

Siler found his true calling in real estate. He did one deal—got in and got out. And got set up for life.

A great aunt had left Siler fifty-three acres in Randolph County, North Carolina. It was an uninspiring parcel of clay and rubble in the rural Piedmont region of the state.

Because the land wouldn't perc, it could not accommodate a septic system.

"No perc, no house," the guy at the county office said.

So, Siler couldn't build on it. He couldn't sell it to a developer. All he could do was pay the fucking taxes every year and curse his great aunt for leaving him the burden. The neighboring property owners laughed at him.

Liquored up one night, Siler found the solution.

He would start a pig farm. Or at least announce that he was starting a pig farm. With the waste lagoons, oppressive stink, noise, and environmental hazards, pig farms had become the ultimate NIMBY villain.

No one, and I mean no one, would tolerate talk of a pig farm in their part of Randolph County. It didn't matter that the county may never issue a permit for such an enterprise. Siler banked on the idea that simply announcing his intent would so outrage the neighbors that they would buy his land—just to get him out of the county.

Give him credit. Siler made the play in a big way. He got the high school band out to his property by pledging to contribute to the booster club. He catered the event—pork barbecue, of course. He invited the county commissioners and the extension agent.

And on one sticky hot morning in August, Siler announced that he was bringing a pig farm to his Randolph County land.

Someone threw a trumpet at him. Siler erected a tent on the land and began sleeping there nights. He bought three little pigs and fenced them in on the property. Put up a big sign announcing the arrival of Three Little Pigs Farm—"coming soon."

The sheriff had to post a car by the property out of concern for Siler's safety. The Greensboro newspaper heard about the kerfuffle and sent a photographer down. Siler sold the idea hard, focusing on the "job creation" opportunities in a depressed area of the state.

Then, the big pork politicians in DC—the men and women paid by the pork lobby to fight for every pig farmer in America—heard about the story and adopted Siler as their celebrity case. Why, they argued, any private landowner oughtta be able to make an honest living raising pigs. A famous Opry star showed up at Siler's patch of clay and sang 'Proud to be an American' for the cameras.

Within sixty days, an attorney representing a collection of neighboring landowners came out to the tent to see Siler. It was 3:00 a.m. on a Tuesday. Very quiet. Very serious. Delivered a one-time, take-it-or-leave-it offer: End the media circus. Take down the signs and sell the property, on the spot. Sign on the dotted line without taking a breath, right there under the tent. Or get ready to face legal bills that would bankrupt him.

Siler signed. The attorney handed over a check for five times what Siler had been hoping for.

Forty-eight hours later, Siler had purchased a spot in Chapel Hill. Within a month, he opened Pig Farm Tavern.

There was a small stage at one end of the bar. Siler hosted open-mic nights and student bands a few times a month. He also did exclusive shows with musicians coming through town. He would sell 100 tickets for anywhere from $100 to $1,000 per person, using the event as a fundraiser for the labor association representing the housekeepers on the UNC campus. Those housekeepers have always been the most abused, put upon employees on campus. Siler had a soft spot for the housekeepers, based on his tenure in Connor Dorm. Over the years, his events spun off millions of dollars in donations for the men and women who clean up after the kids.

At the other end of the bar, there were three booths.

In the middle was the pool table.

The place was long and relatively narrow, like a shotgun house swollen up to the size of a bar. There were seventeen stools running down the patron side of the bar.

Siler, a man of simple brilliance, stocked seven varieties of beer, seven choices of liquor, and seven wine options.

He claimed it was a religious requirement. He usually had about a dozen pimento cheese sandwiches in a beer cooler – ones he picked up from Merritt's store around lunch time. For friends of the bar. Time Out was the catering choice for late-night patrons. And Crook's Corner on Wednesday's for barbecue.

During the right time of year, he kept a tin of persimmon pudding in the beer cooler by the sandwiches. Siler's wife made the deserts by hand, including the pudding. She used fresh Chatham County persimmons.

Siler was on his third marriage. All to the same woman. Siler and Carla both had roving eyes. Gave each other a lot of leeway. So it was never clear just where the line might be found.

When Carla crossed the line enough, Siler divorced her. It was five years into the marriage.

Within eighteen months, they were married again. A decade later, Carla filed for divorce. Wrote in the court papers that Siler was "deficient as a man, beyond what can be captured by English language sentences." No one disputed that.

Two years later, they reunited at a Merle Haggard show. Siler was hanging backstage with the guitar techs and invited Carla along for the evening. Story was, they fell into a deep kiss when Merle was singing "Yesterday's Wine." They seemed to have found some equilibrium. No one forecast a third divorce.

Today, he was settling up the NFL betting pool from the past week.

"You know, Lassie. This is supposed to be a friendly little pool. Everybody kicks in two bucks, and the winner gets $50. Where's the harm in that?"

I saw no harm. He continued.

"But I've got a fucking degenerate ruining our setup. Maximillian Whitehall, some stats professor. He showed up at the start of the season and talked his way into the pool. Took a spot that opened up when Mallette pulled out. Fucking stats guys all think they've figured out a system."

"Now he's running all these side bets and parlays with my guys. Five of them pulled out of the pool last week. Said they couldn't take the pressure. Pressure? How is two bucks pressure? They told me they had gotten tangled up with Whitehall on these wacky bets. Most were winning money off him, but it was ruining the games for them. He's relentless in begging for the action, but then he won't pay up. Apparently owes money all over town."

My soup was done. "So you banning him?" I asked.

"Yep. Today. Getting ready to send out an email to everyone on my list. Putting the scarlet letter on Whitehall. He'll never place another bet in this town again," Siler said.

And like that, Whitehall was toast.

Chapter 9

Someone forgot to tell the groom,
the biggest secret in the room.

She was the first girl that he kissed,
the first perfume he missed.

First to light his flame,
the first girl to sing his name.

But she gave herself away,
before she ever learned to play.
Now she can't get away,
too soon.

everal folks around town used Pig Farm as shared workspace during the afternoon hours. Siler provided free Wi-Fi and coffee hot enough to kill germs.

I moved over to one of the back booths with the laptop from Fats and printouts from a few of the GRL files.

Working from absolutely no basis of information, I had to find Bootstrap and figure out what was behind the daily allegations of fraud.

Or I could go another way and try to find the fraud. That might, or might not, lead to Bootstrap's identity. But focusing on the fraud seemed the fastest way from here to there. If I could wrap this up early, I could get the million-dollar bonus and celebrate.

A year-long gig working for Fats would be lucrative. But also god-awful stressful. And I am, by nature, lazy and averse to stress.

So, I decided to skip a couple of steps and seek out evidence of fraud.

To do this, I decided to create a kind of test.

More than 100,000 individuals worked for GRL as employees or contractors—or as authors publishing through GRL research publications.

In theory, I would subject each individual to a lie detector test. Abracadabra, the results of the tests would point me to the fraudster. Or, if no one failed, Fats could conclude that Bootstrap's emails were harassment and a hoax.

The Pentagon might be able to pull off this methodology.

I could not.

So, I decided to create a kind of reverse test. Instead of interviewing more than 100,000 individuals and analyzing the results, I would start with the results and work backward.

I started with a checklist of variables that would be most likely to show up in a test of fraudulent activity:

- Authors whose publications had swung quickly from mediocre content (or rejected content) to newsworthy articles

- Employees who had been either passed over for a promotion recently or received a big promotion

- Employees who recently were linked to litigation

- Employees with big swings in personal finances

- Employees with recent real estate transactions

I spent the next couple of hours poking around in the GRL administrative platforms. All of the web pages covering employee benefits, employee assistance programs, staff policies, and so on. My login gave me administrative access, so I could also slice and dice files from the private Human Resources portal. At its most detailed, the database contained individual records on every one of the 100,000-plus individuals who might be the source of fraud. With their Social Security numbers, I could link their GRL files to all kinds of data from industry sites that carried out credit checks and background checks. GRL had contracts with many sources of these data, which meant I had found a way to keep this moving.

The idea was to throw all 100,000-plus individuals into a giant sifter, that shakes and sorts every entry, using the variables above as a screen. I was confident most of the individuals would pass on through.

Every individual would receive a score of 0, 1, 2, 3, 4, or 5 based on the number of variables in the screen that showed up alongside their name. An individual not tied to any of the variables would receive a score of 0 and pass through cleanly.

Individuals hitting on every one of the variables would receive a score of 5.

I would start by telling the sifter to hold on to only the individuals with a score of 5. These would be people with a lot of volatility in their lives, of late. This would give me a pool of people posting the highest possible score on my test. So, I would be starting with the results, then doing some reverse engineering to figure out the story of how and why each person had been retained by the sifter.

I ran the methodology by Siler.

He shifted, put the coffee in his right hand, and leaned on the bar with his left elbow. Dumb look on his face.

"I'll ruminate on that," he said.

I closed the laptop and zipped the GRL backpack. Woke up my personal phone and punched up the TouchTunes app. Played most of the double album Townes recorded in 1973 in Houston, *Live at the Old Quarter*.

Siler had run lighting and done some work as a guitar tech for Townes in the late 1980s, when we finished up school in Chapel Hill.

Townes was closer to the end than we knew. Siler was along for the ride on the 1990 tour with The Cowboy Junkies.

From the jukebox, Dale Soffar wrapped up his opening announcements on the live track, then "Pancho and Lefty" came on. We had about twenty songs to run through before "Tecumseh Valley"—a tune that always makes Siler tear up just so.

"Nice," Siler said. Dumb look on his face.

"Hey, almost forgot," Siler continued. "LTD Mel and Panhead Mark are coming through town on their annual east coast tour. Said they had two shows in Durham and would stop by for a pop. You got a song to pitch? Or you tied up with Fats tonight?"

"Fats is on a plane for New York. Or will be, any minute now. She's meeting with investors and doing a *Today Show* gig early tomorrow."

"Then we'll make a night of it right here," Siler said.

He handed me a pimento cheese sandwich.

Chapter 10

Magnetic pull, like the moon on waves.
Caught in the tide, can't pull away.

High risk, low return.
Falling knife, never learn.

Bite of the apple, live for today.
Eternal judgment, it can wait.

She's a bad decision in a strapless dress.
She steals from Santa and the IRS.

I put the sandwich aside, for later. Started a new mug of genmaicha tea. So hot, the steam was making my cheeks moist.

I opened the laptop again and logged into my UNC account to go through notes and questions from Mallette about my doctoral defense.

The PhD had seemed like such a big deal twenty-four hours ago. It was the culmination of this phase in my life. It would be the stamp of approval from academe. Which means absolutely nothing. Except that it does mean something. Just nobody knows what. And it means something different, for sure, now that $5 million is on the table.

I could hear Mallette's admonishments over and over.

"The best dissertation is a completed dissertation," he would say. "Your dissertation is not the best thing you're going to write. It's merely the first thing you're going to write."

Mallette had held appointments in the Department of Sociology and in the School of Journalism. He was unusually gifted. Through his career, his research findings would generate a scholarly article, a mass media column, and, in some cases, a textbook. He could write in all three styles for all three kinds of audiences, and he drew on both quantitative and qualitative methods. He was the leading voice on the role of media in society – on the right side of history from Watergate through Fake News.

Mallette was seventy years old, but the only real choice for the post of chancellor. Given the athletic and academic fraud in recent years, the university trustees ultimately had no choice. They had to select someone who could lead the campus out of the dark period. They waived whatever mandatory retirement rules were in place and begged Mallette to take a five-year contract. His job was to disinfect the campus and make the job attractive enough that a national search would be practical by the time his contract ran its course.

My dissertation was relatively straightforward. I was extending the research on agenda setting—a body of theory and evidence that, in short, held that the media don't tell the people what to think. But media do tell us what to think *about*. I was drilling into the model to measure the White House's influence in telling the media what to write about.

Most everything was in place. I was a week away from the defense. Not a lot of work left to do. But some loose ends. And I couldn't focus.

This morning, I had deposited the first check from Fats, for $1.25 million, into my checking account at the State Employees Credit Union. Just went through the drive-through window and handed the clerk the signed check and a deposit slip.

I could see through the smoked glass window that my check triggered some meetings. But soon enough, she sent the receipt back through the tray.

I was, for a tick of the clock, a millionaire.

Tomorrow, I'll write a check for roughly half that amount and send it to the IRS. As a freelancer, I've always had to send in my estimated tax payments. Same thing here. Just a bigger number.

Numbers big enough that it's hard to concentrate on the time-series statistics I would need to explain next week.

But the millionaire status couldn't compete with Fats. She filled my mind.

She was back in my life, and she took up most of the oxygen. She's the smartest woman I've ever known. She's the best-looking woman I've ever seen. Not everyone agrees—she has her share of haters on social media. But when she's in my presence, or in my head, she trumps most everything else.

I can't get out of my mind the image of those sweat beads on the back of her neck this morning, her white skin visible under her pony tail.

All I could think about was whether I would end up as anything more than an employee. A friend? Ex fiancé? Something more? Less?

Somehow, the $5 million didn't matter when there was the chance, however slight, that I might kiss her again for the first time in thirty years.

My GRL phone buzzed. A text from her. Then another. Then two more.

"Landed at Teeterboro"

"Headed to see hedge fund guys. They love GRL."

"Have you found Bootstrap yet?"

"Roker says hello. He says you should be embarrassed that Battle Park kicked your ass."

Then silence. All I could think about was Fats falling asleep on my shoulder in the planetarium, during astronomy lab, freshman year.

A new text buzzed in: "Is it OK to miss you?"

Wow. What would Townes say here?

"You can miss me for the sake of the song," I texted back, pulling a line from the steamy night in the Old Quarter in 1973.

"Save me a biscuit," she texted. And then radio silence. I'd see her next on the *Today Show*.

Time to switch from tea to rye. Signaled over to Siler.

I closed my notes on Mallette's questions. The defense prep could wait. Or would have to wait. I couldn't focus on anything but that ponytail dancing through Chapel Hill.

Unwrapped the pimento cheese sandwich. God, the sourdough bread is perfect.

Queued up some LTD Mel and Panhead Mark on the jukebox. Maybe I could sell a song tonight. Panhead boomed through the speakers:

> *On the edge of Livingston and desperation.*
> *Tracking neighbors' faces at the heating station.*
> *There must be an America between excess and deprivation.*

I had been playing around with a song about a special kind of woman. One who is both a Baptist and a Communist.

For now, it's kind of half a song. Or part of a song. Hoping it's just the right kind of thing to pitch to LTD Mel and Panhead Mark.

Chapter 11

Empties line the Pearlwood bar, a blind man shoots tequila.
The tourists leave in taxicabs, tweaked out by the dealers.

Buenos dias, mi amigo, have you seen my friend?
Have you seen the pretty girl who taught me how to sin?

Mexican topaz, she shimmers at night.
Her skin is electric and gives off white light.

How many stars in Boca del Rio? How many stars in old New Orleans?
How many stars in Nuevo Laredo? How many stars in Sweetwater Springs?

How many stars can fit in the sky?
How many stars in Brownsville tonight?
How many stars in Brownsville tonight?

*T*uesday evening in October. Sitting at the bar at Pig Farm Tavern in Chapel Hill. 8:37 p.m.

Having moved from the back booth to the bar, Siler and I were screwing around with a new song. Or lines that might, if we got lucky, turn into a song.

Siler had skills, and he was on his game tonight. Leaning against the bar with his left arm. Coffee in his right hand.

"Snow days," he said, as if it were the most obvious way in the world to start a conversation.

"What about snow days?" I asked.

"Everyone needs a snow day now and again—a day when you steal a free day," he continued. "No appointments. No bills to pay. Just free time. You wake up one morning, and, boom, you get a snow day. No school. No work. No nothing."

That rang a bell for me. I remember the excitement of a snow day as a kid. Having my dad open my bedroom door and tell me school was called off for weather. Translating that to a bonus day for a grown man—now that's got real song potential.

We noodled around with ideas and kept pouring rye, kept waiting for LTD and Panhead to show up. Kept the mood going by filling the jukebox with their songs. We cycled through "Heartbreak on Brucemont Drive" three or four times, amazed by the lyrics these two guys put together.

"Not sure 'Snow Day' can compete with that," I said.

"If that's the bar to clear, we can stop writing," Siler said. "But everybody needs a B-side. Let me text LTD to see where they are."

It was getting late, and we weren't getting any smarter. Timing was good to pitch something to the guys.

"Well, shit," Siler said, looking up from his phone. "Those Texas hillbillies are in Durham, all right—Durham, New Hampshire. I told Panhead he owes us a chance to pitch a song, having stood us up tonight like a bad prom date."

Siler took a gulp of coffee and then a sip of rye.

"So what do we have?" he asked me. I was the one working at the laptop to organize lyrics.

"How you gonna pitch a song from here to New Hampshire?" I asked. "Neither one of us is going to sing this into a phone."

"We'll text a few lines at a time. Panhead is at his phone now. He says he'll take a look. What do we have?"

"Start with the title: 'I Need a Snow Day.'"

We fed him a few lines at a time.

> *I can't say I don't have care in the world.*
> *I'm driving carpool for junior high girls.*
>
> *It's she-said and he-said and bubblegum rap.*
> *There's a Jamey Johnson CD I want to unwrap.*
>
> *There's gotta be a better way.*
> *God I need a snow day.*
> *Just a little time to play,*
> *I Saw the Light.*

Siler worked the text editor. Hit send. Didn't wait for a reply.

"What's next?"

> *Grievous Angel with the sunrise.*
> *Whiskey River sharp at noon.*
> *Folsom Prison happy hour.*
> *Then crank up Dublin Blues.*
>
> *The honey-do list is eating me up.*
> *Got a Ray Wylie CD waiting out in my truck.*
>
> *Where are Pancho and Lefty when a man needs a drink.*
> *Kenny Powers is laughing as I fix the sink.*

"Really?" Siler asked. He stopped texting. "You're going with the Kenny Powers line?"

"It makes me laugh," I said. "Tell him Kenny Fucking Powers knows the difference between Durham, New Hampshire, and Durham, North Carolina."

Siler went back to the keys.

"Any more?" he asked.

"Repeat the chorus. Or repeat anything. Shit, I don't want to pretend to tell those boys how to write a song."

Siler was quiet, staring at his phone like he was willing a pot to boil. "Naked From the Neck Up" came on the jukebox, and I was amazed again at LTD's talent with lyrics.

Siler's phone buzzed. He looked up from the text.

"Panhead wants to know the name of that biscuit place you like so much. He's hungry," Siler reported.

"Well, there are a couple. But they're both 800 fucking miles from where he's sitting right now. How long has he been on the road this year?" I asked.

Dumb look on Siler's face. Waiting for an answer.

"Tell him the place is called Time Out, and it's open twenty-four hours a day. Ask him if he wants a song about biscuits."

Siler worked his phone some more. He looked up.

"Panhead says LTD likes that we mention Folsom in the song," Siler reported. "But that we should pitch this one to a boy band. Or to that TV talent show, Teen Idol."

Siler looked down again when a new text buzzed in.

"LTD wants to know if it's true that you have a song about a chick who's a Baptist and a Communist. He's going to be pissed off if he doesn't get first look at that one."

Okay, perhaps the night isn't lost.

"Oh, and Panhead says there's never been a good song about biscuits. And if there is going to be one, it's going to come out of Texas, not Chapel Hill."

It's a hard life out here.

Chapter 12

I'm planting Christmas trees, one leg down the hill.
Sixteen hours away from home, and I am working still.

The sun is rising overhead, and the water pail is dry.
There's a long blue ridge above the trees, and it stretches to the sky.

𝓑 ack at the Gimghoul Road guest house just past midnight, I tried to reorganize my schedule for Wednesday before going to sleep. But I wasn't going to be able to sleep, anyway. I sent myself an email with a to-do list.

Three big items for Wednesday:

1. Run my analysis on the 100,000-plus GRL names and see how many people scored a 5 on my test.

2. Focus for a couple of hours on my dissertation defense preparation.

3. Mail a check for $625,000 to the IRS.

I was awake. I had a stamp, and worked the list in reverse. Wrote the check. Printed and signed the estimated tax paperwork. Sealed the envelope. Walked out to Gimghoul Road, past the big silent Coulee sedan in the driveway, and dropped the payment in the post box.

I was no longer a millionaire.

I could see Orion in the north sky. Fats's new house was dark. Footlights illuminated the stone pathway past the big house and around to my place. The cold air felt good.

I got back to the desk and checked off my item number three. Then, remembered I did have another task to do, and added it to my list.

4. Watch Fats on the *Today Show*.

About four hours of good sleep. I woke up at 5:00 a.m. My alarm buzzed at 5:03 a.m. I'd never had a drink of whiskey in the morning, but I wanted one, then. Seemed like the only thing that would ease the pain of losing half my fortune overnight.

I put my hand on the bottle of Bulleit Rye. I ran my finger across the green label. Swallowed hard. Decided to go with the tea, instead, knowing lunch would come along soon enough. Put water on to boil. Texted Fats.

"What did Bootstrap say today? Please forward me the email," I wrote.

"Quiet this morning. No email from Bootstrap. Has the brilliant Lassie James solved this case already?" she texted back.

The genmaicha tea was good. I queued up Emmylou's album *Red Dirt Girl* on my phone and set it to play on a loop. Opened the laptop to get back to the GRL work.

My GRL analysis was simple. It was the data cleaning that was tedious and time-consuming. I had to append files, concatenate files, and create crosswalks between unique identifiers for 100,000-plus individuals in multiple databases.

I started with the primary Human Resources portal and created a clean database all of the HR information in one place, tied to each individual's record. This covered the hiring date for employees and nature of the relationship for contract workers, consultants, and authors. It covered any HR events, including pay raises, promotions, disciplinary events. I included anyone who had worked for GRL over the past year. For some individuals, the firing or resignation date was included.

Next, I linked this up to the database of GRL publications. GRL publications included everything from peer-reviewed scholarly journals to online blogs. Some of the most obscure, sophisticated science in the world was published through GRL outlets. This required large editorial staffs, networks of peer reviewers, and researchers hungry to publish. There were also pop science publications tied to multi-media GRL outlets that had exploded in the past year.

By matching up author names to publication histories going back five years, I created variables that tracked the number of submissions and whether the submissions were accepted for publication or rejected. From this, I was able to create a variable for each researcher who had submitted content. The variable would sort researchers into three groups. One group I labeled "Consistent"—this grouping included researchers whose publication track record had held steady. A second group I labeled "Supernova"—this grouping included researchers whose publication track record had soared. For example, a researcher would land in this group if he or she had received rejection letters from third-tier journals five years ago but now had headline-making articles in the most competitive journals. GRL's media arm issues news releases for the most eye-catching articles published, in large part to spoon-feed the news media a layman's translation of the science. Authors whose articles received this kind of treatment leapt ahead in their careers instantly. A third group I labeled "Ambersons"—this grouping included researchers whose publication track record had withered.

I was interested in any kind of big swing. But most of all, the Supernovas. Assuming fraud, not sour grapes, was more of a danger to Fats, the Supernovas were researchers who could be trading on false data for personal gain. Someone from the Ambersons pool could be pissed off about the arc of their career. They could be harassing Fats. But if they were cheating, landing in the Ambersons pool meant that they were doing it poorly.

Having linked up the HR data and publication information so I could match up every individual record, I connected this to online security services that performed credit checks, background checks, financial reports, and so on.

Just before 7:00 a.m., my phone buzzed with a text. Fats was at the NBC studios.

"See you on the television in a half-hour," she wrote.

Then: "Roker asked if it's true that you have a song about a woman who is both a Baptist and a Communist?"

"Ask him if he's buying songs today," I wrote back. "Tell him there's a bidding war for this one."

I turned down Emmylou and turned on the TV. Found the *Today Show*. Used it as wallpaper, while I kept cleaning up the GRL databases.

Chapter 13

I became a country DJ,
Learned the songs of Willie and Merle.
Worshiped at the Church of Hank,
Then I heard the Red Dirt Girl.

The grievous angel haunts my sleep.
Shows me the devil and the deep blue sea.
I fell in love with Emmylou.
I don't know what to do.

Wednesday morning in October. Guest house on Gimghoul Road. 7:29 a.m.

The *Today Show* comes back from a local weather break, and a host I did not recognize is seated across from Fats. Some guy. He and Fats are both in white leather chairs. She is wearing all black. Her black hair is down. Her skin glowing.

TV Guy with the smile introduces her as "the first celebrity scientist of the twenty-first century."

He doesn't call her Fats. He says, "Dr. Holly Pike is a modern-day combination of Albert Einstein, Jonas Salk, and Marilyn Monroe. You're inventing designer medical treatments that improve our quality of life while finding cures for disease in developing nations—all while landing on *People* magazine's list of most beautiful people and inspiring a generation of young girls to pursue science."

His first question: "Aren't you setting yourself up for a fall, being all things to all people?"

Fats smiled.

"My blessing is timing. I learned breakthrough scientific techniques at a time in history when technology allows us to transfer this work from the drawing board into real-life applications. And for some people, all I represent is a cure for baldness. Would you like a prescription?"

TV Guy, laughing.

"Not today. But your treatment for baldness is what I'm getting at. How do you balance time and money invested in a cure for baldness with time and money invested in curing deadly diseases? And how do you balance either one with a shoot for *People* magazine?"

Fats, now serious.

"I'm the face of Gimghoul Research Labs, but working with me are more than 100,000 really smart, dedicated people. I can't do it all—and would never try. But together, we can make this work add up to more than the sum of the parts. At any speck on the globe, at any time of day, we have a GRL lab somewhere in the world working on a solution that will make somebody's life better tomorrow than it is today."

TV Guy, leaning forward.

"So what's the highest priority for you, personally, across all of this work? I know you're in New York meeting with investors. What are you focusing on?"

Fats.

"Today, Gimghoul Research Labs is announcing a global partnership with Tickle. Over the next year, we will be rolling out a series of SyNaptz innovations that give people more information about their health than ever before—and, more important, innovations that give people more control over immediate solutions. The SyNaptz innovations will marry consumer technology with state-of-the-art science."

From there, TV Guy poked around more to get information on SyNaptz. Fats mentioned "trade secrets" a couple of times and kept to the talking points. In a flash, the *Today Show* was back to weather.

My phone buzzed with a text from Fats.

"So?"

"I can hear the investors writing checks now," I wrote back. "GRL + Tickle = cash."

"See you tonight," she texted.

Then: "Can we get biscuits?"

No need to reply. Fats can get whatever she wants.

Muted the *Today Show*. Turned up Emmylou. Went back to my GRL data. I had to carry out some test-runs of the analysis, using small random samples of the data. These tests would reveal any glitches in coding and any failed linkages between the disparate data sets.

Once I find, and tie up, all of these loose ends, the first cut on the analysis should move in a hurry.

Chapter 14

She writes me letters about places she's been.
She stopped off in Paris, and she's going again.
New England in spring, then it's Europe for fun.
Drinking wine by the liter, and soaking up sun.
She's seeing the world and making dreams true.
It reminds me I'm here, and I'm missing her, too.

I needed a change of scenery and needed a spot without a beer tap or a whiskey well.

For the first time in many years, I dug out my key to a carrel in Davis Library and spread out to prep for my dissertation defense.

Immediately, I did what every grad student does in a carrel. Went fast asleep.

At 4:30 p.m., my phone blew up. The buzzing nudged me awake.

Two voice mails from Mallette.

Fats had called four times and texted six. The first messages were playful.

The last one, not so much.

"You do work for me, correct?" was all the text said.

Mallette said he wanted to catch up tomorrow after the University Day celebration wrapped. Nothing about my defense, he assured me. Something new, related to a faculty matter, where he said, "I would benefit from your expertise."

Right behind it, there was a second voice mail from him: "Let's meet in The Pit," he said, referring to a gathering spot at the center of campus. "October is my favorite time in Chapel Hill. All meetings should be outside."

I called Fats.

She was at the Gimghoul Road house. She didn't find me at the guest house. Siler reported I was not at Pig Farm. And she did not welcome the mystery. She wanted a report on Bootstrap.

I told her I would have a first report by Friday. That seemed soon enough.

She was heading to Pig Farm. Told me to meet her there.

I said, sure, give me one hour.

I spent the time going through my notes from Mallette, for the dissertation defense, which was now less than a week away.

This would be the first doctoral defense anyone could remember chaired by the sitting university chancellor. A defense is usually a private academic meeting of no interest to the community. This one, however, was of great interest. I would be seated with Mallette and other members of my committee on a stage in Gerrard Hall, one of the oldest buildings on campus.

Gerrard sits next to South Building, location of Mallette's new third-floor corner office.

The university community was invited to attend. It was more of a celebration of Mallette than an affirmation that I would clear the bar to take a PhD. Which was fine with me. Put all the spotlight on him.

I had to be ready to explain my use of a methodology known as "autoregressive integrated moving average"—or, for short, ARIMA modeling. The method helped me determine whether the White House was setting the agenda for national news media or whether the reverse was occurring.

I had to explain how my work advanced the body of knowledge in "agenda-setting theory," a question that extends back to the rise of mass media in the twentieth century. The scholarly testing of agenda-setting ideas dated back to the 1968 presidential election, when researchers in Chapel Hill gathered evidence of the news media's influence over voters.

In the end, the public nature of the defense should help me. I would hope that having a student meltdown at a doctor defense would reflect poorly on the committee members themselves. It was in their interest, as well as mine, that it all go well.

That rationalization would have to do.

I headed to Pig Farm.

Chapter 15

Flip flops pass for magic slippers, at the beach house at Lahaina.
Sunblock scrambles GPS, so the office cannot find you.

The clocks are frozen like the drinks.
Stuck on Happy Hour.
Fading fast bikini strings,
Stuck on Happy Hour.

*W*ednesday afternoon in October, bleeding into evening. Sitting at the bar at Pig Farm Tavern in Chapel Hill. 5:02 p.m.

I'm at a back booth, laptop open. Multiple GRL databases running. I briefed Fats for about forty-five minutes, giving her an explanation of my methodology and explaining why, for now, this approach is better than others.

She asked 100 different questions. I could see the CEO wheels turning. She challenged me to articulate multiple scenarios of what might happen and how we would proceed from there. As a scientist, Fats lived in a world of bright-line findings. As a CEO, she knew there really were no yes-or-no questions. It's more about how she managed feedback and found opportunities in whatever situations materialized. She refused to be locked in to a single course of action that limited her options.

By 6:30, Fats was racking up the pool table. Nine-ball. For some time, she kept peppering me with questions, even as she knocked balls around the table.

When that faded, Siler made a biscuit run. We ate at the bar. I was on my second mug of hot tea. Siler was jacked up on coffee.

From her bag, Fats pulled a 1963 bottle of Macallan. Set it on the bar. Spun the bottle around for us to see.

"We're celebrating, boys," she said. "Tomorrow, I get one of those fancy academic gowns and hoods and get to sit up on stage with real-live scholars. There was a time, mind you, when we were all in Connor Dorm not knowing how to get through drop-add."

Siler pulled three glasses from the overhead rack.

Fats poured.

"It's good to be home. Too much history between the three of us to spend any time . . ." Fats paused, her voice trailing off into a silent, personal recollection.

"Just too much time," she repeated.

Siler lifted his glass, as a toast.

"To 'too much time,'" he offered.

Glasses clinked. We put the whiskey to our lips. Siler poured his coffee in the sink. 1963 Macallan allowed no companion.

"Who's performing tonight?" she asked.

"Jefferson Hart," I replied. "Local guy. Great talent. Has a new hit with 'Marigold.' I'll send you the video."

"He's on at 10:00," Siler said. Switched from leaning his left arm on the bar to his right. Dumb look on his face. "You hanging around?"

"Not tonight," said Fats, finishing her whiskey. "I have a video conference with Tokyo later. Heading to Mallette's residence now for a reception with other honorees. You boys are my excitement for the night. The Macallan is yours. My gift to you. Squares us for thirty years of neglect."

Fats kissed me on the cheek as she got up from the barstool. It was so quick and familiar. I wasn't sure if I dreamed it or if it happened. She waved goodbye over her head as she walked away.

Siler poured me another one. Poured himself another one. It was going to be another long night.

A couple of beats after her exit, Fats opened the door and stuck her head in.

"Oh, yeah—you still owe me a link to that song about the Baptist and the Communist. Tomorrow night," she yelled. A directive, not a request.

She was gone again. Off to rub shoulders with donors and scholars.

I finished my biscuit. Siler threw her half-eaten meal in the trash.

"You not going to Mallette's?" he asked me.

"What? And leave you here alone with the Macallan?" I said.

Then: "Nah. He invited me, but I passed. It's her night."

Jeff came in the back with a couple of guys and began tuning guitars and testing the mics. I punched up "Marigold" on the jukebox. He came over to catch up. Turned out, he's playing a bill with LTD and Panhead in Atlanta next week.

"Tell them they owe me one," Siler said, relaying the life lesson about Durham, New Hampshire and Durham, North Carolina.

"Panhead sent me some lines from 'Snow Day,'" Jeff said.

I waited to gauge his reaction.

"Good stuff there, Lassie," he said, returning to his guitars. I took another sip of whiskey, bolstered by the admiration of a successful songwriter.

"Should make a great video for some Teen Idol contestant," Jeff said, laughing.

Well, so much for "Snow Day." I guess everything will be riding on the Baptist and the Communist.

Chapter 16

She loved Miss Patt and Blue-Eyed John, cranking lonesome whippoorwill.
Now on Key Biscayne, she dreams about it still.

Dreams about the Ryman, roaring Rocky Top.
Banjo angels haunt her sleep, choruses won't stop.

She's the Queen of Whiskey Glam. Jack Daniel's meet Kate Spade.
She always wins at Twister. She played the Turf back in the day.

*J*eff played late. We drank late. He performed a set of Tom Petty covers and got a lot of the pretty girls up dancing. Rare to see dancing at Pig Farm. Girls in jeans and boots can turn any surface into a dance floor.

Several of the dancing girls closed down the place. Siler left the bar a mess, locked the door, and invited a few of us back to his house in Carrboro. On a lark, I tried the number in the GRL phone for the black car. It was there in six minutes.

"Grilled cheese," he announced when we entered his place.

Siler had the place to himself. Carla was up at their Valle Crucis vacation home, where the Pisgah and Cherokee national forests connect in the mountains. Carla spent as much of the season there as she could, meditating under the spell of the mountains and hosting an autumnal equinox get-together for friends. It was spiritual. Every fall, with Carla reviving her emotional self, Siler hosted a series of late-night bacchanals to overwhelm his physical self. He was quite good at it.

I dialed up Tom Petty tunes on my phone and plugged it in to Siler's system.

Like all good late-night parties, the energy level settled a bit. Two of the girls sat down at Siler's coffee table and cranked up a game of checkers.

Siler's neighbor, Sam, who always showed up for late-nights, came in the back door and opened a bottle of Grgich fume blanc. Siler put thick slabs of Velveeta on rye bread and got the sandwiches sizzling on the griddle. I sank into a burnt orange overstuffed chair and watched SportsCenter with the sound muted and the closed captions turned on. Jeff came by with his bass player.

Siler brought me a sandwich, and I tore off bites of the charred bread and dripping cheese, stuck in a trance between drunken sleep and conversation.

I dreamed of the defense next week, sitting at the round table in Gerrard Hall and having Mallette and the committee pass the cover page of my dissertation around and sign it. Which would confer the PhD.

I chatted up the checkers girls without hearing anything they said in response. For one of them, I read her palm. Something I learned at a New Orleans solstice party years ago. Told her how her love line would lead her to happiness in a frigid climate or take her on a journey of sadness and love loss in a warm city by the water. Palm reading is all about giving the client choices. Palm reading isn't about destiny. It's about giving the client permission to imagine options she didn't know existed. She told me she'd buy a coat.

Fats did that for me. When I was with her, I imagined doing things that would not otherwise occur to me. Everything seemed possible with Fats. Even gravity became optional when Fats was smiling at you.

My mind ran off to the GRL analytic models I was getting ready to run. Could I find the needle in the haystack? I liked the feeling of depositing GRL million-dollar checks into the credit union, from the drive-through window.

The only thing better is filling out a deposit slip for song royalty checks. I had been hoping to pitch John Prine on "She's a Baptist and a Communist." I hear it in his voice. Had a fuzzy conversation with Jeff about recording a demo.

Perhaps a new song about reading palms.

That dizzy feeling was winning. Put my head back on the big chair. Closed my eyes. Left the checkers girls to contemplate arctic love versus tropical pain. I faded away, a former millionaire, full of whiskey and Velveeta, uncertain what lay ahead. A week ago, my course was so certain. Now, chasing Fats around the world sounded more fun than anything else. Unless I could get more Texas musicians to record my songs.

Jeff picked up a guitar and sang the acoustic version of "Marigold." It was the last thing I heard before the world changed.

Chapter 17

Say a prayer for all the ghosts,
who cannot find their home.
Wandering the Boulevard,
condemned to cry alone.

Say a prayer for travelin' mercies.
Say a prayer for misspent youth.
Say a prayer for all the lies you told,
and all the people that you used.

Thursday morning in October. Sitting at the bar at Pig Farm Tavern in Chapel Hill. 9:07 a.m.

Whatever comes after numb, I was experiencing it. Everything I ever knew, the last three hours tossed it out the window.

Chapel Hill police were banging on Siler's door at 6:00 a.m. Mallette's executive assistant, Rose Bynum, knew I would be there and sent them.

Rose had arrived on campus early. University Day required all hands on deck. She was ready.

Rose parked at the planetarium, by the sundial, and looped through McCorkle Place on her way to South Building. Taking the brick walkway just south of the empty slab, where Silent Sam used to stand, now a stain on the University's reputation. She tasted bile every time she thought about the Klan members assembling on campus to praise the icon. More than ever, Rose felt a pull toward the less famous monument on the prized quad – the marble obelisk marking the grave of former University President Joseph Caldwell. All the more reason to turn her back to the Silent Sam scar tissue cordoned off by metal barricades.

Her thoughts made the connection from Caldwell to Mallette. Two great leaders. She wanted a great day for Mallette. For his inauguration. For the university that was desperate for his leadership.

When she turned by the memorial, she saw something out of place. Some kind of mass. No, a body. Clearly now, a body collapsed at the south base. She ran to it. Rose crumbled when she recognized Mallette. Minutes later, she was able to dial 911 on her cell. Sirens woke up the town. News helicopters followed. Within an hour, the governor had postponed University Day. The University's Board of Trustees convened an emergency meeting.

The police fetched me because Rose said I was next of kin.

Every stage of grief hit me at once. I was angry at everyone and no one. I didn't believe it. I sobbed. I slammed my hand against the table. Given that I'm not, in fact, a blood relative, I had to scramble to find a contact for Mallette's daughter, Pearl. She was in Maine. His wife passed three years ago.

The Chapel Hill mayor immediately called the FBI. I heard whispers. This was no heart attack. There was something like a knitting needle rammed into the base of his skull.

My old editor from the *Post*, J.C. Houston, called me and asked if I would write a piece.

"Soon. Maybe. Not yet," I said, and hung up the phone.

Siler opened his place as sort of an unofficial hub for friends, and law enforcement made the spot a command post. Every booth was occupied. Every stool, also. Enough computers and monitors to make the place look like a TV production studio.

Rose had been admitted to UNC hospitals, suffering from shock.

Fats texted me when she saw the breaking news on the CNN crawl.

"Is it true?" she asked.

"Yes," was all I could write. I did not elaborate and could not.

I was still in my Wednesday night clothes. Sitting at Pig Farm and waiting to be interviewed by a state investigator. A block away, on the quad, several thousand students and local residents had gathered. The crime scene was taped off. On the periphery, the people gathered began singing "Amazing Grace." I could hear the collective voices from the upstairs bar where I sat.

I thought back to my sophomore year, when I landed in Mallette's newswriting class. I didn't know anything about newswriting. Worse, I was ignorant of the severity of my deficit. The only good thing, Mallette said, is that I had no bad habits to break.

"You have no habits at all," he said. It was never easy to tell if he was smiling.

Mallette taught us AP Style, where to put the commas and where to put the semicolons. Writing an AP lead was like learning to bake a cake. Follow the rules.

He also taught us more. Mallette challenged us to question how we know what we know. We signed up for journalism. He taught us epistemology. Getting an expert sound bite was never enough. Even finding a statistic from a reference librarian was not enough. On the continuum of absolute ignorance to fist-pounding certainty, Malette demanded, figure out where you are sitting when you tell the public that you know something.

Mallette gave every one of his students laminated cards, small enough to fit in a wallet.

On one side of the card was printed the North Carolina open-meetings law. We were taught to hand that card to any public official who tried to close a meeting.

On the other side of the card: "Comfort the afflicted, and afflict the comfortable."

Mallette, whose own reporting had freed five innocent men from death row, lived that every day. The university faculty had become comfortable. Too comfortable with mediocre academic performance and outright fraud, in some departments.

When Mallette agreed to take the corner office in South Building, a lot of us believed those comfortable people were about to feel some affliction.

I heard my name.

"James Battle?" a voice asked.

A man approached on my left. Dark suit. White shirt. Red tie. Wingtip shoes. Hair cut above his ears and the smell of 1955 shaving lotion.

"Inspector Gerald Pauley," he said, offering his right hand.

We shook.

"Call me Gerry," he said.

Then: "Who paid you $1.25 million to kill Mallette?"

Chapter 18

You'll find him on the front porch swing.
Whittling stick and Pearl in the can.
He runs the county from that porch,
like he was chosen God's right hand.

I froze.

I'm certain I gave off a million cues of guilt. I was anxious to speak to the FBI or state investigators, or someone. We had to catch Mallette's killer. Nothing else mattered.

Now, in the span of five or ten seconds, I was processing all the variables that probably put me at the top of the list of suspects.

I couldn't speak.

"You taking the Fifth?" Pauley asked. "Didn't figure you for a coward. At least not right out of the box. Everyone tells me you're a smart son of a bitch. Don't you want to try to outsmart me?"

"Detective . . ." I began.

"Inspector," he corrected.

I took a breath. Drank more tea.

"Inspector," I picked up, "thank you for getting your team out here this morning. I need you, the University needs you, we all need you to catch whoever killed Mallette. I did not kill him. I did not kill anybody. Let's talk this through so you can devote your energy to more productive leads."

I stopped.

Pauley looked at me. Didn't speak. Didn't blink.

"Gimghoul Research Labs paid me $1.25 million. Fats—uh, Dr. Holly Pike hired me to carry out research. That's the reason for the money. Has nothing to do with Mallette. I'm on the payroll. Dr. Pike will confirm that."

"I have three questions for you," Pauley continued.

I nodded.

"One, why is your name all over Mallette's calendar?" he asked.

I explained that I had been working with Mallette for three years. I was a doctoral student, and he was my advisor and my committee chair. We were old friends, with a student-mentor relationship that developed into a friendship as time passed. While Mallette was a professor, I had worked as his research assistant. With Mallette becoming chancellor and my dissertation defense next week, we were meeting regularly. Our last meeting was about planning for the defense next week.

Pauley kept staring at me.

"Oh, he invited me to his home last night, for the reception with University Day honorees. I did not attend. I was here with Siler,

Jeff, and others. Slept at Siler's house, after we closed here," I said. I assumed he wanted an alibi.

"What about today's meeting?" Pauley asked.

I rewound conversations from the past couple of days. Finally remembered the voice mail from Mallette.

"I was working in Davis Library yesterday. Mallette left me a voice mail asking to meet today, after the University Day events wrapped. He asked to meet in The Pit. Said it was not about my dissertation. Something about wanting my input on university business," I said. "That's all I know."

"Second," Pauley rolled on. "What are you doing for GRL?"

I gave the Inspector a superficial summary of the assignment from Fats. That she hired me, essentially, for an investigative reporting job. To figure out if any of the researchers are using the GRL publishing outlets to line their own pockets. I didn't mention the harassing emails from Bootstrap. Waited to see how much detail he demanded.

"Third," Pauley said. "What do you know about a person or a project named 'Bootstrap'"?

I swallowed. I wanted a shower. I wanted more whiskey. I wanted Mallette to be alive and to protect him. Or to be far away from here and forget it.

"I don't know anyone named Bootstrap," I said.

Pauley had that look on his face, like Siler. He didn't blink. He didn't smile.

"But you're the second person this week to ask me about Bootstrap. It came up when Fats—Dr. Pike—hired me. One of the reasons she suspects research fraud is occurring at GRL is that she has received emails alleging the fraud from someone using the name Bootstrap. It's not clear if the emails are revealing authentic fraud or if the emails are merely sour grapes, or harassment," I said.

I explained that I had been on the job for only a couple of days, and I had been focusing on ways to detect fraud—if it exists—through the GRL publishing platforms. I had not done anything to pursue Bootstrap.

"Have you spoken to Dr. Pike?" I asked.

"Hate to use a cliché," Pauley said, "but I'm asking the questions here."

"Yes, sir."

Chapter 19

You can't touch it, you can't see it.
But you can't help but feel it.
When the mountains kiss the history of the sun.
There's a spirit at your fingers,
when you close your eyes it lingers.
It weaves in through your heart, it is the one.

$\mathcal{P}$ auley's tone changed. He went from chilling to curious.

"So what do you think Bootstrap means here?" he asked me.

"Until this morning, I had been assuming that Bootstrap and the GRL fraud, if it exists, may not be related. I thought it likely that the name was a random handle for whoever was sending Dr. Pike the emails. Less of a code or signal than a mask. A mask that's both convenient and meaningless. My priority, for the GRL job, is to find the source of any research fraud," I said. "I don't think the person sending the emails was committing the fraud."

Pauley signaled to Siler to pour him coffee. He took the stool beside me. His look invited more.

"With what you're telling me now, my guess—and it's only a guess—is that Dr. Pike spoke to Mallette about the problem. A recent email to her from Bootstrap raised the potential of telling Mallette about the supposed fraud. Dr. Pike and Mallette had grown close in recent months as Fats—I mean, Dr. Pike—got more re-engaged with the University. The school, obviously, saw dollar signs when she entered the picture. I'm sure the fundraising guys were turning cartwheels when she came back into town."

"What exactly did Mallette say to you about the meeting he wanted today?" Pauley asked.

"His voice mail said not to worry – nothing to do with the dissertation defense. He said there was a faculty matter he wanted to discuss, and 'I would benefit from your expertise.' I remember that line because it made me laugh. The guy had more expertise than anyone I knew," I said.

"In his desk calendar, Mallette had your name written down for 3:00 p.m. today, in The Pit. Beside your name, he had written 'Bootstrap' and underlined it twice," Pauley said.

I hoped his willingness to share the information was a sign of trust. And an indication that I would be helping him solve this—not about to be arrested.

"This is new information," I said, and it changes things in both directions. "For me, it means there is some connection between Bootstrap and the UNC faculty. It also means that we should pursue some connection between Bootstrap and Mallette's murder."

"We?" Pauley interrupted.

"The most important thing right now is that I help you find the killer," I said.

"Tell you what," Pauley said, wincing from the bad coffee. "You keep cashing million-dollar checks. Keep studying for your big test next week. Keep writing your songs. I'll do the investigating."

I'm exhausted. I'm in shock. I'm scared. Now, I'm pissed off.

"Am I a suspect? Because if I am, it's an indication to me that you're wasting your time," I said.

"When the chancellor of the University of North Carolina has a knitting needle jammed into his skull in the middle of campus, everyone from the President of the United States on down is a suspect," Pauley said.

He continued with the questions.

"Tell me about Mallette's morning routine."

"I'm sure Rose told you—or would have told you. I'm not sure how much she was able to speak to you today. Mallette was up very early every morning and went running on campus. Or used to go running, when I first met him. The last few years, his jogging had turned into walking. He would be out for walks at 5:00 a.m. or so. Sometimes, he'd invite students out for the walks. I've been with him a few times. Lots of people have," I said.

"Did he walk the same route every day?" Pauley asked.

"Not precisely. But it's a small town. There are only so many routes to walk," I said. "No matter where you're headed, most folks end up going past Silent Sam at some point. Whether they know it or not, the same route takes them by the Caldwell memorial."

"Have you spoken to Dr. Pike today?"

"Only a brief text message," I said. "She asked if it was true, that Mallette was murdered. I said yes. It's all coming apart so fast, I can't imagine what's happening in South Building."

"Coming apart?" Pauley asked. "What do you mean?"

"Mallette's inauguration as chancellor was scheduled for today. He'd been on the job just a few weeks. Donors and big-shots, like Dr. Pike, are in town for University Day. Now, the chancellor is dead, and helicopters are flying over campus. It's the worst kind of crisis, because the guy who would be able to lead us through something like this is gone," I said.

Pauley sat still. Didn't bring another question right away. We could hear the crowd singing a block away.

"Another cliché," Pauley said, sliding his business card down the bar to me. "Don't leave town."

He put a wilted dollar bill on the bar for the coffee. Got up from the stool and headed for the door. Grabbed his coat from a pile stashed on top of the bar.

"One more thing," Pauley said, turning back to me. "I hear you're writing a song about a woman who is a Baptist and a Communist?"

I had nothing for him on this one, and I said nothing. Just held the mug of tea and gave Pauley one of Siler's dumb looks.

"That's a twofer—blaspheme and treason all in one song," Pauley said. "Send me the link."

Chapter 20

Guess things happen this way.
Doesn't dry my tears.
Guitar town, and Dublin blues.
It's a hard life all these years.

The grievous angel haunts my sleep.
Shows me the devil and the deep blue sea.
I fell in love with Emmylou.
I don't know what to do.

*F*ats walked into Pig Farm as Pauley was wrapping up. I saw the two of them huddle. Conversation was brief. He hugged her. He left. She walked toward me.

Fats was wearing a Navy blue suit that looked like tiny electric lights were sewn into the fabric. Something she might wear to ring the opening bell on Wall Street—something she probably has done a dozen times. Her black hair was TV perfect. Her cranberry lips oozed against the white skin.

Siler met her at the opening in the bar. They hugged.

Off my barstool, I hugged her as she approached.

"This is as bad as it gets," she said in my ear. "I've dreamed of hugging you again, but never imagined it would hurt so much."

She squeezed me.

"So what do you know?" I asked. "I see Pauley gave you a hug, not the third degree, so I'm assuming you are on the inside of this one."

"Let's see," she said. We both took barstools.

"The chairman of the University board of trustees is announcing an interim chancellor in just a few minutes. It's the law school dean, Porter."

"He'll be fine," I said.

Jones Porter was born a Vermonter but moved as a teen to the North Carolina Outer Banks. He was a bundle of affects, part New Englander, part Southern professor, and part Hatteras Island. Whatever he was as an attorney, and I had no idea, I knew that he was beloved personally on campus.

"I was with Mallette last night, as you know, so I called the FBI this morning and offered the assistance of my GRL security team. Pauley has a couple of my guys helping to secure Mallette's office.

"The national media have flipped out," she continued. "This is like the O.J. car chase and the Boston bombing rolled into one. East Franklin Street is closed to traffic and occupied by satellite TV trucks. And it's going to get worse."

"What happens next?" I asked. I couldn't process how we could overcome the emotional grief to operate the University, though clearly the machinery must run.

"Lots of things," she said. "I'm just coming from a meeting with Porter. He had a private talk with all of us who'd come in for University Day honors. Unbelievably painful. The University is canceling classes today, and a wave of cops and state and federal agents will be on campus. The absolute No. 1 concern is security—there is a killer free, and no one is sure if the place is safe. Was Mallette targeted? Was this random? Is it the start of some killing spree? Is it terrorism? Every scenario is on the table."

"You know," I said, "Mallette would be mad as hell at this disorder. He despised mobs and thugs who disrupted civil discourse and the democratic enterprise."

"I remember," she said. "His reputation on that point lives on. There is a fierce debate going on now about canceling classes. Obviously, the University is closed today. The security issues alone require it. But are classes canceled tomorrow? If so, for how long? Porter is working with the FBI and the governor's office on that. And the White House, truth be told. The fear of liability is driving the decision making for now."

I remembered Bootstrap.

"Hey, do you know why Mallette would have Bootstrap beside my name in his calendar?" I asked. "Did you take up the GRL business with him?"

She let out a laugh.

"Why do you think I hired you?" she asked. "I ran the problem by Mallette a couple of weeks ago. Tried to hire him. He said to hire you. In fact, his exact words were: 'James Battle is better at finding needles in haystacks than anybody in the country.'"

"Mallette had asked to meet today and said it was about University faculty business. Did he mention a connection between the prospect of GRL fraud and faculty here?" I asked.

"No, never," Fats said. "Lots of University faculty have published through GRL outlets, but that's the same with every Tier 1 research university in the world. I'm guessing that our conversation about GRL fraud prompted him to want to revisit whatever system the University has to discourage research fraud. After the athletics and academic fraud crisis here, the last thing he needed was questions about the integrity of the research done on campus. And he would have had his eye out for it."

My adrenaline was gone. I was out of tears and out of luck. I needed a shower and a bed and a prayer that somehow peace of mind would come again. I couldn't imagine that it ever would.

"A couple more things," Fats said, putting her hand on the back of my neck to pull me back into the conversation.

"Porter wants to keep your defense on for Monday," she said.

"What the fuck?" I interrupted. "Has he lost his mind?"

"Hold on," she said. "Think about it. Your dissertation defense was already a public deal. Having a sitting chancellor chair your committee was a big deal—at least among the insular group of academics who care about cranking out PhDs. Now, it's a national event. Everybody cares, the *Today Show* included. Keeping the defense date will be a public demonstration that the University is back open for business. It will be a tribute to Mallette. A real honor for him, to have the last student he advised complete his course of work. That's you."

Fats explained that Porter suggested that we place a chair at the table for Mallette but leave it empty. We would proceed with the dissertation defense with four of the five committee members. And the defense might be moved to Memorial Hall to accommodate the crowd.

"So here's the plan. Saturday morning is a private, graveside service for family only. The old cemetery on campus. Monday is your defense, which begins to put the University back in business. Sometime shortly after, there will be the public memorial service for Mallette. That will be in the Smith Center and will be televised. The White House is reworking the president's schedule so she can speak."

Fats paused. Checked her watch, then her phone. Then her watch again. She was about to be on the move.

I pulled out my phone. Found the number for the black car. Requested a pickup at Pig Farm.

"Last thing," she said. "I'm flying out to New York. Now, in just a few minutes. I'll be back on Saturday to pick you up. You'll be coming with me to Atlanta for the weekend."

I gave her Siler's dumb look.

"It will do you good to get out of this town. The circus is in full swing out there on Franklin Street. You can prepare for your defense from a suite in the Four Seasons. And I'll buy you biscuits from West Egg Café."

Siler walked toward the door. He was talking to a cop. I waved goodbye as we finished up.

Fats was two steps ahead of me through the bar and down the steps. Her high-end Coulee was in front of my black car. Hers still as dirt. Mine idling.

I opened the car door for her.

She hugged me again.

"It's going to get better," she said. "Because you're strong enough to make it better. A whole lot of people will be looking to you for the leadership that they used to get from Mallette. I know you'll step up."

I didn't want to be a leader. I didn't want to be anything.

Chapter 21

My fax machine works fine, and my telephone has wires.
Google is still baby talk, and Velcro is for liars.

Keep your new rules. I like it old school,
want my news on paper and my chicken on the bone.
Keep your new rules. I like it old school,
like to drive a clutch, and rock in chairs at home.

Thursday evening in October. At the guest house on Gimghoul Road. 8:27 p.m.

Lights off. TV off. Not even music. Spent the afternoon somewhere between sleep and nightmare. Would doze off and then leap up when the horror reel went through my mind, again.

Phones off. No interest in voice mail.

A knock on the door.

I kept staring at a dark ceiling. Might as well be infinity.

Another knock. A tap on the window.

It occurred to me that Pauley would probably use more intrusive methods. So, I got up, flipped on the light, and opened the door.

I caught my breath at the sight of Pearl Mallette.

She was in worn blue jeans, black turtleneck, tan boots. White raincoat and hood. She didn't say anything for what felt like a full minute. I tried not to sob. She looked like a lost puppy.

"I had nowhere to go," she said, finally. "Dad always said you would know what to do if trouble showed up."

"Your father was generous with his praise," I said, "among many other things. Come in, please."

I waved her in. Hung her coat on a hook on the back of the door. We took up spots on sides of an L-shaped sofa, our eye line creating a hypotenuse connection across the empty space.

I had not seen Pearl in more than a year. I had spent a few Thanks-givings with her and her father. I had been at three or four university functions where she was present, and we had once sat a row apart at a symphony performance. I remembered that she was recently divorced. No kids. Splitting time between Chapel Hill and a place in Maine her mother had treasured. Pearl worked as a genealogist, doing research for private clients and consulting for the booming TV family history shows.

But I had never been in a serious conversation with Pearl Mallette. Certainly never had a personal conversation.

Her dad might be the only thing we had in common. Or not. I had no idea. I had no idea what to say.

Words started to tumble out. A series of sentences that amounted to non sequiturs. As if my voice alone would cure pain.

"Would you like something to drink? It's good to see you again—well, not *good*, of course. Did you speak to Inspector Pauley? Would you like some food? How did you know I was here?"

Pearl cried and smiled at the same time. She reached across the hypotenuse and put her right hand in my left.

"Can we just sit here for a while?" she asked. "I've been talking with law enforcement, university suits, and all kinds of people nonstop since this morning. I'd just like to sit for a bit. To sit somewhere I feel safe. And I feel safe here."

She released my hand. Sat back in the sofa. Closed her eyes. The muscles in her face and neck softened after a while.

Pearl was like a golden Aspen leaf—more beautiful than ever before freeing itself from its binding. Before sailing to the ground. This was the moment that divided her life into two parts. Like her dad, she was big in the moment.

Part one was everything up until the call from Pauley. Part two would be her life going forward without her dad. Pearl would forever have two acts in her life. I was sitting with her during the most private moment–what amounted to a brief intermission before the second act became real. Sitting on the sofa with me. With no one asking anything of her, about her. No one asking why this all happened. No one asking rhetorical questions that would cause her shoulders to droop and her neck to cramp.

"Some music?" Pearl asked, eventually, not even opening her eyes.

I plugged my phone into the audio system and scrolled through options. Saw a Doc Watson link and remembered how thoroughly

Mallette liked his music.

Clicked on shuffle. "Columbus Stockade Blues" came on.

I got up and put a kettle on the burner. For tea.

Chapter 22

She makes up songs about the sun and moon,
and she sings to them in the sky.

She keeps the lighthouse burning blue,
and never asks God why.

I drank tea. I drank whiskey. Alternated through the night.

I watched Pearl sleep.

She stretched out on the long arm of the L-shaped sofa. She used a cushion for her pillow. I put a fleece blanket over her. Removed her boots without jostling her too much.

Well into Friday morning, I reconnected with the electronic universe.

On the GRL phone, two texts from Fats.

She was cranking through New York business, with financers. She was reading obits of Mallette. Never seen anything like this, she said. Confirmed that she would stop off at RDU on Saturday, for me to meet her there. We would spend the weekend in Atlanta, then get back to Chapel Hill for my Monday afternoon defense.

Second text: She reported on back-channel conversations with Porter. Fats would lead a campaign to honor Mallette and kick it off with something like a $100 million gift. Wanted to hear my ideas on how funds would best honor Mallette.

I wrote back: "See ya Saturday." Acknowledging receipt of her notes but agreeing to nothing.

I switched over to the browser and looked for Mallette obits.

The New York Times had multiple breaking news stories on the murder, the search for the killer, implications for other university presidents who might be targeted by terrorists now focused on disrupting American campuses. Then, there was the obit.

It was chilling.

> *CHAPEL HILL—University of North Carolina Chancellor Sanders Mallette was found dead on the heart of campus here early Thursday morning in what federal and state authorities are investigating as a homicide.*
>
> *Mallette, 70, was stabbed in the back of his neck with a sharp implement akin to a knitting needle that penetrated deep into his skull, according to law enforcement officials with first-hand knowledge of the crime scene.*
>
> *Mallette was found before dawn, face down on the ground beside a landmark on the oldest part of the campus, where buildings date to the 18th century and 200-year-old trees cover the quad. His body was less than 100 feet from the temporary stage set up for his own inauguration, which was to have been held later that morning.*
>
> *Mallette's executive assistant, Rose Bynum, had arrived to campus*

early to prepare for the day's events and found him as she walked to her office in South Building. Mallette was wearing athletic gear, and law enforcement officials believe he was killed while on a regular early morning walk.

A former journalist and an accomplished scholar who held chairs in the University of North Carolina's sociology department and in its School of Journalism and Mass Communication, Mallette was the recipient of two Pulitzer Prizes for reporting that freed five innocent men from Death Row.

Mallette managed a rare balance of newspaper reporting and scholarship. He earned a bachelor's degree in music in 1967 and then a master's and doctoral degree in sociology, all from the University of North Carolina. During a newspaper career that took him from The Mountaineer in Waynesville, NC, to The Washington Post, Mallette also built a record of scholarship in sociology by exploring poverty, crime and the structural inequities that, he believed, led to the headlines in daily newspapers.

At a White House event in May, Mallette accepted the Elaine Lewis Medal, awarded by the National Academy of Sciences every five years in recognition of unparalleled research in the social sciences.

Mallette moved quickly through junior level reporting positions, reaching the Post by age 32 and winning his first Pulitzer in 1980, at age 35, for a series of stories that ultimately freed three African-American men from Death Row in Pennsylvania.

Shortly after, Mallette left daily reporting and took up writing a column for the Post and teaching at his alma mater. He received his second Pulitzer Prize in 1984 for commentary that examined the social networks of Texas prosecutors and judges involved in death penalty cases that resulted in questionable convictions. The sociology research and the journalism fed one another for this reporting, and Mallette was appointed to an endowed chair in the university's sociology department following the Pulitzer award.

Following three decades in his roles as professor and journalist, in August Mallette accepted a five-year appointment as chancellor of the nation's first state university. The appointment was heralded by faculty as a positive step toward reversing a long-term, damaging athletic and academic fraud scandal.

Mallette was to have been inaugurated Thursday during University Day ceremonies that mark the laying of the cornerstone in a building that is now known as Old East dormitory. University Day ceremonies were canceled.

Sanders Arthel Mallette was born March 3, 1945 in Deep Gap, North Carolina, sharing a birthday and hometown with the legendary folk musician Doc Watson, who grew up with Mallette's parents in the North Carolina hills outside of the town of Boone.

Deep Gap influenced Mallette in ways that set his life course. Immersed in music and the church, Mallette first planned to attend the seminary before enrolling in the University of North Carolina and pursuing an undergraduate degree in music. Through his graduate work in sociology and his scholarship in this field, along with his work in journalism, Mallette continued to examine how music and faith are intertwined with both urban and rural poverty.

In one of the most cited sociology tracts of the last generation, Mallette's research showed that music played nearly identical roles for the poor, white children in the rural town of his youth and for the disenfranchised African-American youth in poor U.S. urban neighborhoods of today. Serving as both a coping mechanism and an anchor of identify that could not be taken away by authority figures, who were not trusted within the communities he examined, Mallette re-framed the way white leaders and African-American leaders viewed culture.

As a legacy to his work, an annual music and cross-cultural event showcasing bluegrass, folk, and Americana music alongside rap, blues and gospel, is held annually. The festival alternates between locations in Appalachia and in urban venues.

My tea was cold. The whiskey was warm. It was 5:00 a.m.

I took a shower and worked through all the stories Mallette had shared during the year I was in his newswriting course. He had just won that second Pulitzer. I was a curious kid who could write a hell of a lead but didn't know a thing about what came in the second graph.

Mallette taught me that and more. It was as if lighting had struck and created new circuitry in my brain.

I got back into jeans and a *Post* sweatshirt and went back to check on Pearl.

Like her father, she was beautiful.

Chapter 23

The yellow brick road is cracked.
The peach trees never bloom.
The Bible Belt is full of lost souls.
They will cross that river soon.

*F*riday morning in October. In the guest house on Gimghoul Road. 6:03 a.m.

Pearl stirred.

It rained most of the night. In the last hour, the rain had stopped. There was not a sound outside.

Pearl sat up. Coughed. Wiped her eyes. Smiled.

"I'm hungry," she said. "Never did have anything to eat yesterday. Never thought I would want to eat again. But I do. I'm hungry."

"Let me try something," I said.

Picked up the GRL phone. Punched the number for the black car. Answer on the second ring. Pearl grabbed her pocketbook and pointed toward the short hallway leading to the bedroom and a bathroom, raising her eyebrows as a way to ask for directions. I nodded and pointed. She headed toward the hall.

"Hey, James here," I said.

"Yes."

"Can you run down to Sunrise Biscuit Kitchen and bring us some chicken biscuits, bacon-egg-and-cheese biscuits, and some cinnamon rolls?" I asked.

The bathroom door opened. Pearl stuck her head out: "and coffee."

"And coffee," I said. "One. Large."

"On my way," the black car said.

I clicked off the phone and folded Pearl's blanket. Fluffed the cushion back into sofa form. Lined up her boots to the corner of the coffee table. Checked my iPhone and saw more than 200 unread emails in the past twenty-four hours. I highlighted row after row and deleted them all. I heard the bathroom door open again. She was back.

"Who was that?" Pearl asked, nesting back into her spot on the sofa. "You can't take your big Coulee out of the driveway and get us breakfast?"

It was good to see her smile.

Pearl had done a quick scrub of her face. Her cheeks were flush from the rush of water. She was reassembling her pocketbook, putting a toothbrush and hairbrush down alongside her pocketbook. Her shoulder-length blonde hair was wet and brushed hard and flat.

"I wouldn't know how to turn the thing on," I said. "Coulee belongs to Fats—uh, Dr. Holly Pike. You may know her. Founder of GRL. Big shot. Your dad and the development staff have been courting her for a donation to the University."

"So then who's running your breakfast errands these days?"

"Tell you the truth, I don't know who it was I called," I said. "Just a guy in a black car who answers the phone when I call. You can thank Gimghoul Research Labs."

"Dr. Holly Pike again?" Pearl asked.

"Yes."

"Heard a lot about her from Dad. Met her once when I was at a New York event with him. Hadn't thought about her in ages but saw her on the *Today Show* the other morning," Pearl said. "Good to know she's handing out drivers."

"I'm doing some consulting work for her. Long story. Boring story. For another day," I said.

"I look forward to another day," she said.

Pearl noticed me eyeing her sparse personal supplies.

"This is my luggage—all of it," she said, and shrugged. "When I got the call in Maine, I left with what you see me wearing now, and what I could throw in this bag. The lights in the house are still on, I expect."

I couldn't bear to discuss with her the life-stopping trauma of the phone call informing her of her dad's murder. I went back to her question about my call to black car.

Got up to put more water in the kettle for tea.

Room went quiet. The only sound was the gas range humming.

"Put some music back on," she said. "Some of yours. Dad always talked more about your music than your Pulitzer."

I had put together a playlist of artists performing songs I'd written. Had never played it for anyone, but I had it in the phone for my own peace of mind. Scrolled through to find the list on my phone. Clicked on it, and Jeffery Dean Foster came up first, singing about that brunette.

"I know there's no blueprint on how to handle what's happening here. I don't know how to process the facts, and I can't bring myself to speculate. But I want to do whatever I can do to help you today, tomorrow, and then one day at a time," I said. "Do you have any idea what today will bring—for you?"

Pearl explained that the FBI was treating Mallette's South Building office as a crime scene—all of South Building, for that matter. In fact, the FBI essentially viewed the entire north campus as a crime scene. While it couldn't rope off the entire campus, at least not literally, the FBI had placed more than 200 state and local cops, plus some FBI agents, across the spread of north campus, from Spencer Dorm to the ROTC building.

"Same for the chancellor's residence," she said, referring to Quail Hill, the university-owned residence offered up to the sitting chancellor. "He was only using the place for university functions and entertaining. He was still living at his house—our house."

Mallette had kept his personal residence, a Queen Anne house on Friendly Lane. FBI agents were stationed there, also.

"I told the FBI I was holding the graveside service Saturday—that's tomorrow now, I guess. And they should have the autopsy done by then. I'm not waiting for these folks. Dad is gone. I don't have any interest in hosting long receiving lines," Pearl said.

Her mother had passed several years prior. Pearl was an only child. The weight of a public mourning period would fall on her, entirely.

"What does Pauley say?" I asked.

"The FBI guy?" Pearl laughed. "Not much of a bedside manner, but I trust that he'll catch whoever did this. I take him seriously. He wanted to fast-track the autopsy, no surprise. So, I expect he and I are on the same page."

I poured boiling water into a mug with two genmaicha tea bags.

"He says I'm a suspect," I said, scared that Pearl might hear this first from Pauley and take a different and hostile view of me.

Pearl laughed.

"He says I'm a suspect, too," she said.

Chapter 24

Magdalene Laundries and prisons for hire.
Cash machines spitting out dust.
Cyprus is the canary to watch.
It could happen to any of us.

What does the winner win? What does the loser feel?
Is Howard Hughes still rich? Was Apollo Seven real?

The GRL phone buzzed. Black car on the line.

"Two minutes away, sir," he said.

I found a tray and a roll of paper towels and got everything set up on the coffee table in front of the sofa. This was going to be an indulgent pork, chicken, and sugar festival. I was looking forward to it, as a sedative. Sleep had not come to me.

"What's on your schedule for today?" I asked Pearl.

"Well, I owe Porter a call. He has a room for me at the Carolina Inn. But there was so much press outside the hotel, I couldn't bear to walk in there last night," she said.

"Yeah, how did you find me? Meant to ask you last night—I mean, I'm glad you did. But not many people know I'm here. The guest house came with the consulting gig, and I just started this week."

Pearl smiled.

"Siler knew," she said. "Pauley told me I would find you at Pig Farm. He had an agent drive me there. Siler pointed me here, and I had the agent drop me off. guess now the entire federal bureaucracy knows you're here."

I drank a big swallow of hot tea, processing the news that law enforcement and TV cameras may be camped out on Gimghoul Road today.

Pearl picked up the conversation on her own.

"There are two things I have to do today. One is meet with Porter. He was close to Dad. He said to call him anytime today. It's on him to find a way forward for the University, and he wants to hear from me. I don't have anything to offer, but I trust him. I'll call him in a bit," she said.

A knock on the door.

I came back with three sacks, the gooey goodness seeping through the wax paper wrapped around the treats and through the paper bags.

Put everything down on a tray and tore open the bags. Spread out the options on the tray. Waved my hand over the food like Carol Merrill. First choice went to Pearl.

She started with coffee. Drank it black, like her dad.

"The second thing?" I asked.

Pearl opened three wrappers. One biscuit with fried chicken and dripping orange cheese. One biscuit with bacon, egg, and more dripping orange cheese. One cinnamon roll the size of a softball.

She took big bites from each selection.

"My brain loves you for this," she said, her face growing flush from the sugar. "My hips, not so much."

In truth, her hips looked okay in those jeans—better than okay. Pearl was just shy of five-foot-eleven inches tall. She had been a swimmer at Chapel Hill and had kept the long, lean form. Her shoulders were impressive. Her long fingers tore off chunks of cinnamon roll. Her fingernails were painted gold.

I was part way into a biscuit with chicken, egg, and cheese. Pacing myself.

"Okay, the second thing," she continued. "I've got to reconnect with Pauley. He suggested mid-afternoon would be a good time for a briefing on the investigation. Supposed to meet him at Pig Farm.

"Oh, and I have to meet with the funeral home guy. Creepy. He said they would work overnight and coordinate with the medical examiner—or whatever. I just know that I'll be at the graveside at sunrise tomorrow morning for the ceremony. Whether Dad is there or not. They can bury him later if all the details are tied up. But the ceremony is tomorrow."

"The old cemetery at sunrise is what he would like. I know it was a special spot for your dad," I said.

She explained that Mallette had purchased three plots in the old cemetery way back in 1980, when he came into real money after the first Pulitzer. The cemetery dates back to the late eighteenth century and sits on the eastern edge of campus, just a couple hundred yards or so from where we were blocking our pain with melted cheese and sugar. There's not an inch of room left in the cemetery. Plots are sold on secondary markets for a lot of money. They change hands privately and out of public view. Mallette had secured three spots when he had the opening. He was always smart about moments.

"Before Mom died, she made him promise to bury her in Maine. She's got a plot looking out at the ocean. So the three plots here have been empty. One for Dad. One for me, I guess. And we have a spare," Pearl said.

The playlist with my songs was on its third or fourth loop through. I was worried it was overkill. She said nothing about it.

"So I guess that's three things. Porter, Pauley, and funeral home guy," she said.

I finished my biscuit and was working on a cinnamon roll, eating it from the center swirl out to the edges, like every good Tar Heel learns to do. Pearl had finished her three items, leaving crumbs and grease on the wax paper. She wiped her hands on her ass.

"You'll be there tomorrow morning," Pearl said. It was not a question.

Her mom passed. Now her dad. A graveside service for family only. It hit me that this meant Pearl would be there alone, in the daybreak October chill of Chapel Hill. What could I say?

"Yes, I'll be there," I confirmed. "Whatever you need."

Pearl said she wanted to get back to the Carolina Inn and try to sneak in the Cameron Avenue entrance. And she needed some clothes. I dialed up the black car and lined up the ride for her. Told the driver to make himself available to Pearl later that morning, also. Take her to Julian's. She would buy a coat and something to wear tomorrow.

"And you'll be at the dissertation defense on Monday," she said. Again, not a question.

I shrugged.

"It may not matter that Porter wants you there and needs you there," she said. "But I need you there. Dad's last act in his job as a professor was to get you through the defense. You can't leave this a loose end."

I saw then that my resistance to dissertation defense was selfish. It was my personal protest against the horrific crime that had scarred the campus. But my resistance would hurt people like Pearl and draw attention away from Mallette's legacy. I wasn't the story and didn't want to become the story.

"I'll be in Gerrard Hall on Monday, as planned."

The black car was in the driveway.

Pearl stood up. Hooked her pocketbook over her head—the strap on her right shoulder and the bag slung across her left hip. Draped her raincoat over her arm. I stood up. In her boots, she was a bit taller than I was, standing there in my socks. She put her hands on the sides of my face and kissed me on the lips. Two short kisses. And then leaned her forehead against mine so our eyes connected directly. I thought I could see tears forming in the corners of her eyes, and I could feel the same thing happening in mine. Up close, her skin looked like it had been scraped free of all outside elements—no makeup, no crumbs, and no judgment. She had the most authentic, peaceful look I had ever seen on a woman's face, like Grace Kelly staring into the camera in *Rear Window*, dominating Jimmy Stewart with her gauzy look. In arl's eyes, I could see the fierce will of her dad. Little white flecks of fire in the green iris of her eyes. She was tougher than I had ever known—or expected. Her eyes were ferocious, and she said more with her unblinking stare than she could have with words. She somehow made me feel better, communicating to me that not only was it okay to buck up but that I had better do so. Life is for the living—a cliché until you have to face the real loss of a loved one. After a while, it's not cliché anymore. It's how you get up and move on. The tears never came to her eyes. All I saw was beautiful determination and an unreal stubbornness. Not to muddle through. Not to limp along. But to burst through the pain with such force that the world had to take notice. Pearl was good at moments, too.

She kissed me again. Two short kisses on the lips.

"Three things today," I said.

"Three things," she repeated. "I expect I'll see you at Pig Farm later. I want to try that tea."

I opened the door for her. She stepped out onto the stone pathway. The sky was as blue and smooth as cake frosting. Not a cloud anywhere. A heavenly day, arriving just when we needed grace. Pearl turned back and spoke to me.

"Is it true you've got a song about a woman who's a Baptist and a Communist?" she asked.

She blew me a kiss. Actually, she blew two short little kisses.

Chapter 25

Four quarters make a dollar. Ten dollars make a day.
Grilled cheese is a liar's meal, and Dylan sings okay.

Out here in the vineyard, we dance to Emmylou.
I can't find my keys. I've got the Bougainvillea Blues.

*F*riday in October. Sitting at the bar at Pig Farm Tavern. 4:48 p.m.

I had surrendered to fatigue and carbohydrates and emotional pain, and slept the day away. Right in the same spot, Pearl had slept on the sofa. I could smell her hair in the cushion. I could feel her energy emanating from the blanket.

Up at 4:00. Showered in water so hot it hurt. Shaved and brushed and in jeans and a sport coat, I packed up my phones and computer in the backpack. Found my way to Pig Farm. Took the long way around, to avoid the yellow police tape, the candle vigils of professional mourners singing on the quad. Around the TV trucks. Came up Rosemary Street and took the back fire escape up to the door by the storage room.

The bar was full of coffee-drinking law enforcement. Carla was at the front door, keeping tourists and star fuckers out of the place. The

TV cameras made a star of Pauley immediately, despite the pretense he made about staying out of public view. He sputtered boilerplate sound bites into the camera.

Others liked the camera lights more and would make their way down the line of TV trucks, asking if they could offer thoughts—or, better yet, be in a live shot.

One of the blonde talkers from Fox was going live from Franklin Street tonight. MSNBC and CNN had eighteen-wheelers on the sidewalk, with mobile studios hosting live shows all day long. It was professional wrestling's version of the news.

I took an open booth in the back, by a wall outlet. Carla waved. Stuck to her post.

Opened my laptop. Used "page down" and the "shift" key to highlight screen after screen of emails. Deleted them all without reading. That felt good.

Siler brought over a pot of roiling water, just off the burner, with a knot of genmaicha teabags steeping. And a mug.

And a short glass of Bulleit rye with a big cube. Siler loved the big cubes. He refused to put the big cubes in glasses for tourists or students. He wouldn't even tell folks he had a dozen or so a night behind the bar.

He joined me in the booth.

"Fucking circus," he said. Dumb look on this face. "No cop ever paid for coffee, so I'm running a free canteen for America's finest. And nobody but you is willing to come inside and drink in a bar overrun with cops. They gotta catch this guy."

The whiskey was very good.

"Got a sandwich left?" I asked.

"Saved one for you. And some pudding," Siler said. He retrieved both from the bar and put the food on the table beside my computer.

"Pearl was in about an hour ago," he said, "looking for you. She's a little rattled, but only a little. Can't believe how she's holding up. Said she had to go see the funeral home creep. And she'd be back in a bit."

I poured the tea. Gulped down the first hot mouthful.

I mentioned that I saw Jefferson's truck outside. Siler said he planned to try some live music tonight, to break the monotony of the coffee club of cops. Jeff agreed to do a late set, starting at midnight. Siler was promoting it to close friends via email.

"Nothing big," he said, "but I want to see if we can bring back some kind of vibe into this place, something other than a Miranda cluster fuck."

"Cops?" I asked.

"The ones I've asked are all for it. They can't keep up a twenty-four-hour vigil anymore than we can. A break during the overnight shift seems a good fit," he said.

I opened the laptop. Moved slowly through half of the pimento cheese sandwich. There was jalapeño in the mix today. The whiskey was a good complement.

I had decided to go back to emails sent before Thursday morning at 6:00 a.m., to try to pick up where there was some normalcy left off. Truth be told, I couldn't even remember what I was working on before I got the call about Mallette's murder.

I deleted a few more emails from my screen. Now, the most recent emails were those that arrived late Wednesday night and in the early morning hours on Thursday, during the time I was at Siler's place, with Jeff strumming the small Ovation guitar and pretty girls acting like they believed the lies they were hearing.

Among the Wednesday emails was a note I had sent to myself, with my notes and thoughts and work to date on the GRL consulting gig.

I forced myself to get back to that work. Get lost in the data. It was healthier than a sackful of biscuits.

Chapter 26

Used to sell my moonshine,
now I'm buying day-old bread.
It's what happens when the preacher man,
leaves Saluda for Kiev.

*I*t took more than an hour, but I eventually reconnected with the research design I had developed.

I had full access to the GRL systems, all of the data on employee benefits, employee assistance programs, and hiring and firing. Inside the GRL intranet, I found messages back from the company's Chief Information Officer, giving me access to the propriety security databases the company uses to run background checks, credit checks, and more.

By my best count, there were 118,000 unique individuals eligible for my analysis.

It took another hour to develop a query that would ask all of these databases to talk to one another. They spoke a common language, but it wasn't English. I was a novice at the programming code, so I kept running simulations on a small sample of the data to ferret out all the glitches in my code.

I was asking all of the databases to look at several variables at once:

- Authors whose publications had swung quickly from mediocre content (or rejected content) to newsworthy articles

- Employees who had been passed over for a promotion recently or received a big promotion

- Employees who recently were linked to litigation

- Employees with big swings in personal finances

- Employees with recent real estate transactions

When I mastered the code, the computer would follow my direction—literally. It would throw all 118,000 individuals into a virtual colander. Through a sorting and sifting process, the machine would assign every individual a score.

Scores could be 0, 1, 2, 3, 4, or 5 based on the number of hits beside each name. An individual who had not experienced any of the situations in my test would receive a score of 0.

I was an impatient journalist. Not a thoughtful sociologist, like Mallette.

I was gambling that I would learn something from the extreme cases who scored a 5 on my test. If I was right, I'd turn a year-long consulting gig into a one-week victory.

The wrinkles in the coding language kept me from getting the simulations to run successfully.

Another hour went by. I was now drinking two swallows of the whiskey for every sip of the tea. But I was lost in the data—a rationalization, yes, but one I welcomed.

Siler slid into the booth with me and swapped out the old tepid kettle with one still roiling from the burner. A new knot of teabags steeping.

"Shit," I said, hitting another trap in the coding sequence.

"You back on the work for Fats?" he asked.

"Yeah. The data are all there—at least as far as I can tell. But I'm still stuck on simulations with a fraction of the data, trying to get the code to run clean," I said.

Dumb look on his face.

I continued: "You promised me you'd ruminate on my methodology. Anything?"

He took in three mouthfuls of coffee.

"Yes. If you can find a way, I would add in a variable to show professional and personal connections. You've set up a methodology to look at individuals. Adding networks would help you. You don't have thousands of independent actors in the database. You have people who love each other, hate each other, marry each other, and tell secrets to one another. If you know who's connected to whom, you'll find the needle in the haystack," he said.

Dumb look on his face again.

"Mallette used to say that, when you treat a data set like you're looking for a needle in a haystack, sometimes you miss the fact that they're all needles—that there's something special about every case in the file," I said.

I rubbed the fog out of my eyes. Staring at the screen too long.

"Well, you're better at finding needles," Siler said. "He was better at explaining haystacks. You do what you can do."

Siler took his coffee cup and returned to the bar.

After three more simulation runs, I had picked out all the sour notes from the code.

My GRL phone buzzed.

A text from Fats. Said she would see me at RDU at noon tomorrow. Gave me directions to the private aviation hangar and the gate code.

I hit the key to run the test, scouring through all 118,000 associates in the GRL database. One database talking to another database talking to another database, cross-checking unique identifiers for tens and tens of thousands of individuals.

I was logged in to the GRL portal, grabbing time on the GRL servers.

The Pig Farm jukebox started with a burst. Live version of Lyle Lovett's "If I Had a Boat."

Caused me to look up.

Siler's way of jolting me back into lucidity. Pearl was walking into the bar. She spoke to a couple of law enforcement officials, who stood ramrod straight when she walked by.

Pearl shook Siler's hand. And Carla's.

This was as much of a receiving line as she was going to do.

Pearl spotted me. Proceeded past the pool table, down the length of the bar. Past the stools. To my table. Watching her walk was something. Her face brightened as she got closer. The white flecks in her green eyes were lightening bursts.

She slid into the booth across from me.

Picked up my mug of hot tea and drank a big swallow.

"Hmmm," she said. "Not what I expected."

She picked up my short glass of Bulleit rye, with the big cube still holding its form. She drank it dry.

"Just what I expected," she said.

Chapter 27

Eyes from Matamoros, lips sweet as whipping cream.
Met her by the old Cortez, down on Jackson Street.

Brillante like the Southern Cross, reflecting Holy light.
We're leaving for Havana, on a chartered plane tonight.

"*G*ive me a minute," she said.

Pearl closed her eyes. Leaned her head back on the leather rest, at the top of the booth. Clasped her hands together in her lap.

Ninety seconds passed. She was drifting into sleep or meditation.

Siler brought her a mug for tea and a short glass with a big cube. Left a bottle of rye.

I poured my own refill.

Pearl opened her eyes slowly. Wiped her eyes as if she was rubbing away a night's worth of sleep from her lids.

"Self-hypnosis," she said.

I lifted my short glass of rye, offering it as my own version of induction into an altered state. "Self-hypnosis," I said, nodding to my own whiskey totem.

"Ya get there however ya get there," she said.

Pearl poured herself a cup of tea.

"Three things?" I asked.

"Yep. Done," she said. "Just back from the funeral home creep. He's set for burial at sunrise. I declared sunrise to be 7:23 tomorrow morning. So it's done."

Pearl had booked an 11:00 a.m. flight back to Boston. She had rushed away when she received the call and needed to pin down things in Maine before returning to Chapel Hill to deal with her dad's affairs.

She winced at the taste of the tea, but continued to sip it.

"Long meeting with Porter. He's a mess. He doesn't want to be chancellor but knows no one else is ready to step in for Dad. He is 'interim' in the truest sense of the word. His top priority is reopening the University. His second priority is finding a way to honor Dad, to create a legacy on campus."

"Fitting, and it shouldn't be hard. Your dad got us most of the way there with his service to the state," I said.

"Pauley is a piece of work. He'll be graveside in the morning, with us. Porter is there, too. When I catch him being honest, Pauley admits not a whiff of a lead."

One option, she explained, is a random crime. Mallette in the wrong place at the wrong time. A thug happens to cross his path and kill him. That kind of thing has happened in Chapel Hill—but never at 5:00 a.m. on the quad, with a knitting needle. Another option, she relayed from Pauley, is someone who hated Mallette. Everyone has enemies. Problem with this theory is that Mallette's opponents were intellectual, not physical. And they'd gain nothing by harming him. Third option is assassination or terrorism. Feds were working this angle aggressively. A group of analysts was arguing that Mallette was assassinated in a move by ISIS or Al Qaeda to destabilize the country by murdering cultural and intellectual leaders. Just as flying planes into buildings would disrupt commerce, removing university presidents or symphony conductors would tear at the nation's cultural fabric.

Feds had put security in the offices of presidents at fifty prominent universities across the country. And at the Kennedy Center, Lincoln Center, and so on. Feds were looking for "chatter" online, she said.

Autopsy revealed no surprises.

"A standard knitting needle," Pearl said, repeating the gruesome facts relayed by Pauley, "available at any hobby shop or sewing shop. Made of wood."

Jammed into the base of the skull, through the brain, a knitting needle became a killing tool. Mallette fell face first to the ground, landing on the brick hearth that serves as a base for the Caldwell memorial. The needle in the head combined with the blow to the front of his head, when he fell, ended his life.

"So it was someone who took him by surprise, or someone who knew him enough that he allowed them to approach," she said.

Then: "Which puts us right back to square one. No idea if it was a stranger or a friend. And it took some strength, but Dad was seventy years old. It wouldn't take an unusual amount of muscle."

"And the timing?" I asked.

"Rose's 911 call, when she found Dad, was logged at 6:13 a.m. Medical examiner estimates he died at 5:00 a.m. The activity meter he was wearing on his wrist had logged about a half-mile of activity for the day. Which was about the distance from his private residence— our house off Rosemary Street—to the spot where he lay. So they expect Dad was just beginning his walk."

"So he started before 5:00 a.m. that day?" I said.

"Yes, which the FBI questioned at first. But the meter stores data for twenty-one days. They could scroll back and see the activity data from the past three weeks. He frequently logged minutes between 5:00 and 6:00 a.m. There were a few days where he started between 4:00 and 5:00. So it was not as strange a situation, as they thought at first. Not like he had arranged a once-in-a-lifetime pre-dawn rendezvous. This was routine."

Pearl was still in the faded blue jeans and knee-high tan boots. The black turtleneck was gone. She was in a fitted blue shirt with a button-down collar, wool jacket in a purple shade found at Julian's. And a scarf that was a shade or two lighter than the jacket.

Pearl saw my eyes examining the new wardrobe.

"And I have a new dress for tomorrow," she said, smiling. "Thank you for the black car, by the way. That may be the best perk I've ever seen."

She eyed the uneaten half of my pimento cheese sandwich. Perceiving no objection, she reached for it without asking.

"Hey, we can do better than that. I can take you to dinner somewhere," I said.

"Nope. It's safe in here. Remember, I'm looking for safe. The trick is to park myself somewhere safe and focus on what lies ahead, not what just happened. My eyes are on the future."

I drank more whiskey.

"How's the Carolina Inn?" I asked.

"Less of a zoo, but still too much for me," she said.

"So?" I wasn't sure if I should take the lead here, or not.

"So? So? So, I'm going to be back on your sofa tonight. Unless you have another woman booked for the spot already. That's the only excuse I'll accept," she said.

"No, no. Of course, not. Or I'll take the sofa tonight. You take the bed."

"Either way, we can walk over to the old cemetery together, as the sun rises tomorrow."

"Sure."

Pearl finished her tea and winced again.

"I'm assuming that gave me enough anti-oxidants to accommodate a barrelful of whiskey," she said.

She poured her own glass – the amber rye covering the big cube.

Nodding toward my laptop, she said, "What ya working on?"

Chapter 28

The mountain work will leave me weak, and food is days away.
I'm eating laughs and drinking tears, and dancing through the day.

The sunset glitters through the pines, a long day finally ends.
The ragged A-frame shack is home, and dreams of her begin.

Tiler kept the Lyle Lovette rocking on the juke, mixing in some Lucinda Williams, Elizabeth Cook, and Lucero.

I explained the GRL methodology and the general notions behind the consulting gig.

"Like I said last night: Long story. Boring story. For another day," I said, wrapping up an embarrassingly technical lecture to a woman growing more beautiful by the minute.

Pearl did a U-turn with the conversation.

"How old are you, James? Or, it's Lassie, right? Is Lassie James what they call you?"

My face was flush. I sipped the whiskey to stall for time.

"Which question do you want me to answer?" I said.

The woman I almost married, Bianca Lyon—a barrister I fell for when I was reporting from London—hated when I responded to her interrogatories with that question. Absolutely hated it. Once at a white-tie event at The Dorchester in London, she peppered me with three or four questions in a row. When I gave her that reply, she threw a bottle of very expensive vodka through a window. The window was closed at the time. Our row made the London tabloids. That wasn't the end. But, looking back, it was the beginning of the end.

I hadn't thought about Bianca in a long time. If we had met ten years prior, or ten years later, I expect we would have been happily married. People talk about finding the right person. The bigger challenge is finding the right time. We found precisely the wrong time. Our career aspirations made us compete for the oxygen in the room. We both wanted it all. Pearl reminded me of Bianca in one way—she was as fierce. But unlike Bianca, Pearl maintained a quiet ferocity. She communicated the fire through her eyes, not the volume of her voice. I was starting to care about her, and I didn't mean to give her a reason to throw a vodka bottle.

She didn't throw anything. But I wouldn't have blamed her if she had.

"All of them, you idiot," she said.

"Some very old friends, from my undergraduate days, call me Lassie James. And my songwriting credits are generally listed that way," I said. "You may call me anything you want."

"I like 'Lassie,'" she said. She whirled her short glass in a circle, using centrifugal force to spin her big cube around the glass.

"And?" she said. Raised eyebrows.

"Just turned fifty," I said. "You missed my birthday party by about three weeks. Siler and I sat here and ate pimento cheese. Very much like tonight, in fact."

"Well, then, happy birthday," she said.

She raised her glass: "To fifty."

She reached over and clinked her glass to mine.

We drank. We talked over the music, and for the first time, we laughed hard. She told stories about her dad getting into arguments with pointy-headed academics who talked about poverty research at dinner parties. They knew poverty from datasets. Mallette knew poverty from datasets and from sitting with families in homes without electricity or running water.

She laughed at my stories about London. I told her about the fight at The Dorchester—how the wannabe royals ignored my fiancé when she hefted the vodka bottle through the window, high above Park Lane. She laughed at my stories about Fats, about the bands we booked in the old days, hosting all-campus music festivals on the lawn in front of Connor Dorm. She laughed at stories about the dated customs of the graduate school, with all the rules about how the margins of the dissertation document must be formatted.

We laughed until midnight, or nearly so.

Jefferson came in to finish his sound check, before his late set.

Pearl, the voice of reason, suggested we leave. Sunrise was gonna run up on us in a hurry, she pointed out. It was against my religion to walk out on a set of live music, but I knew she was right.

I packed up the laptop and power cord. Punched in the number for the black car. He was there in less than five minutes. He had stored Pearl's purchases from Julian's in the trunk.

We were back at Gimghoul Road and into the guest house before 12:30 a.m. Pearl insisted on the sofa. We repeated the ritual. Jacket on the hook on the back of the door. Boots off. Head down on the cushion. I put the blanket over her.

Set my alarm for 5:45 a.m. and turned up the volume on the buzzer. Closed my bedroom door and dreamed of Pearl in Maine. Walking along the shore in the summer sunshine—the North Atlantic surf still bone-chilling cold to outsiders. In my dreams, Pearl was a transluscent figure bobbing along the shoreline like a shipwreck ghost trapped between heaven and earth.

As the earthly ties weakened, then tore away completely, Pearl floated higher above the beach and then out over the water. The translucent outline of her body dissolved into the clouds, and the sky turned shades darker and twisted into storm formation. In the dream, lightning popped on the beach all around me. I could hear no thunder. See no rain. As I dreamt of sleeping on the sand amid the building storm, I perceived a ghost approach and comfort me with two quick kisses.

Chapter 29

Confronting life and death, failure and success,
moving toward the final journey home.

I am a founding member, of the First Church of Dirt.
I am at my cleanest, when my hands are in the earth.

*S*aturday in October. Old Cemetery on the UNC campus. 7:38 a.m.

It's done.

Mallette is in the ground.

The funeral home creep stayed out of the way. Porter hugged Pearl and cried and shook my hand.

The FBI had essentially made that corner of campus off limits. So, there were no TV trucks. No gawkers. No professional mourners leaving stuffed animals at the grave site.

Pauley hung back, looking grim. But I made a note to thank him for the security. He was looking out for Pearl, and that was a nice thing to do. She was going to pull this off without any press.

At 7:05 a.m., I had walked with Pearl up Gimghoul Road, from the guest house to the old cemetery. She walked two steps ahead of me. Her posture straight, like a swimmer's, and her chin high, like a viscount's. She was in a platinum dress, new black boots. Black wool jacket and gloves that ran up her forearms.

Mallette's plot was on a rise in the graveyard, up high enough to look down on Raleigh Road. The technicians had the hole dug, the casket ready. Before they lowered it, Pearl pulled a Carolina blue bumper sticker from her pocketbook. There was white lettering. She peeled off the backing and stuck it on top of the casket.

"Tar Heel Born and Tar Heel Bred. When I Die, I'll be Tar Heel Dead."

The technician worked the lift to lower the casket into the hole. Pearl threw a handful of old dirt on top, spattering across the casket.

She turned on her heels. Hugged Porter again. Signaled to me that she was ready to depart.

We headed out of the cemetery, back down the slope toward Gimghoul Road. Pearl took my right hand in her left. The leather of her glove felt cold. We walked in step.

Pauley closed in from an angle and met us before we crossed out of the cemetery into the residential neighborhood.

"My condolences," he said, reaching out to shake her hand.

He turned to me.

"Remember what I told you: Don't leave town," he said. He held my look, and his voice made it clear this was not a random comment.

I remembered the plan to meet Fats. Had not even made that connection. This was pissing me off.

"Not to be dramatic, Inspector. I'm grateful for everything you're doing to catch the killer. But I am not under arrest. I am not in your custody. And I'll move about freely, as I wish. In fact, I'm going to take Pearl to the airport to catch her 11:00 a.m. flight to Boston. And I may or may not get on a plane myself. You have my cell number, and I am happy to accept a call from you any time, day or night."

Pauley smiled.

"Tell Dr. Pike hello," he said, walking over to an unmarked FBI car that was idling to keep the heater blowing.

Pearl and I walked down the street, holding hands.

"Dad would have liked that," she said. "He really got pissed off at authority thrown around arbitrarily."

We got back to the guest house. She grabbed her pocketbook and put a tote in the black car.

"You're not escorting me anywhere. I'm leaving now. I should be able to get on an earlier flight," she said. "And you need to get out of here for a few days and get back to work with Dr. Pike. Or prep for your defense. Anything but hang around this town right now."

She said she would try to be back down on Monday, for my defense. Porter had decided that the reopening of the University would be timed to my defense. Upon the commencement of my program, when I sat down with the four committee members, with the fifth chair empty, the University would be open again for classes.

I walked Pearl to the black car, which had pulled in behind Fats' parked Coulee.

I hugged her. She put her hands on my face again and leaned her forehead against mine. She didn't blink. I could see the flecks of lightning in her green eyes—the same lightning from my dreams.

This time, I put my hands on her waist. Then around her back. As lightly as I could manage.

"Are you using your hypnosis power on me?" I asked. Not kidding, either.

"Maybe," she said. "Would you like that?"

"I have never thought about that question until this very second. And I'm going to take a flyer and say, 'yes.'"

"Good," Pearl said.

She kissed me on the lips. Two short kisses.

Then, she vanished down Gimghoul Road, as quickly as she disappeared into the Maine clouds in my dream.

Chapter 30

Why buy when you can rent? Why rent when you can steal?
Don't bother me with interest rates. Just show me my next meal.

Out here in the vineyard, with my patent leather shoes
Turn on the radio. I've got the Bougainvillea Blues.

aturday in October. Thirty-thousand feet in the air. Some-where between Chapel Hill and Atlanta. 1:00 p.m.

Following the directions from Fats precisely, I had rolled through the gate at the private aviation hangar and into the waiting room. Had a bottle of sparkling water in my hand by 12:15 p.m.

Fats was on board. In the CEO chair of the Gulfstream jet painted on the outside with GRL colors. Inside were leather chairs and corporate office furnishings. It was an office in the sky, with a small fold-out sofa in the back for long trips.

Fats was reading financials when I boarded, a phone in the crook of her neck. She gave me the "hold on a sec" wave and motioned me to a leather chair down the aisle from her. From a functional standpoint, it was a chair down toward the other end of a boardroom table—but a boardroom table designed for the sky.

The pilots finished their preflight check. The steward investigated my preferences for drinks, snacks, food, and music. A long way from coach seat on Delta, for sure.

We were down the runway and wheels up before Fats shut down her phone and closed the financials.

The steward had hot tea ready for me. Coffee for Fats.

"What's the state of things in Chapel Hill?" she asked.

Answering her in the form I'm guessing she's used to, as CEO, I kept it simple.

"As of noon today, Mallette is in the ground. Pearl is in the air. Porter plans to reopen the University on Monday, timed to my defense," I said. "The FBI is nowhere on the case—but there are a bunch of agents who imagine this as a new wrinkle in Islamic terrorism."

"The terrorism," she said, "could be as disruptive as 9-11. Attacks that shut down the top thirty universities from the U.S. News rankings would affect millions of people."

"Oh," I said, "and Pauley is ready to arrest me. Threatened me this morning, told me not to leave town. And dropped your name, like he knew my itinerary."

"I'm sure he did," Fats said. "Remember, my guys are helping the FBI secure Mallette's office, private residence, and Quail Hill. My guys would have told him my schedule, and mentioned plans to pick you up today at RDU."

I shook my head.

"Hey, it's Pauley's job to rattle people. He pokes and pokes. People with something to hide crack. People with nothing to hide don't. When he catches the killer, he'll be a hero. Until then, just don't rattle," she said.

I accepted the lecture. Didn't want to make the investigation about me. If I had to take some shit for Pauley to catch the killer, so be it.

I moved to another topic.

"What do you have planned for Atlanta?" I asked.

"Some work. Some play," she said.

"What's the work?"

"For me, it's digging deeper into financials and details about the latest round of capital we're assembling. GRL is on the edge of something really big," she said, laughing. "Put it this way, whatever success GRL has had up until now—we're on the cusp of something world-changing."

"The innovation you talked about with TV Guy?" I asked.

"Yes. And changing the world requires capital. Done right, the science is a magnet for the capital," she said, tapping her finger on a stack of scientific reports. "The work out of our Tokyo office is amazing. We'll have investors in place soon. Then we'll have something to brag about."

"Many millions?"

"Billions," she said. "In multiples."

The pilot updated the weather in Atlanta. Clear and fifty-seven degrees. Landing in a half-hour at DeKalb Peachtree Airport.

"So what's the play?" I asked.

"LTD Mel and Panhead are in town to play a show tomorrow night at Terminal West," Fats said. "I called a friend and booked them for a late show tonight at a little hole in the wall music hall. Starts at midnight at Five Paces."

A midnight show. Roaring Texas troubadour music. Kinda like the old days.

"You better hope there's not an Atlanta in New Hampshire," I said.

"What?"

"Nothing. Too hard to explain," I said.

"And you'll meet Darby," she said.

The steward freshened my tea. I waited for more detail.

"Darby is a partner," she continued.

"A GRL business partner?"

"No. She's a personal partner," Fats said. She looked at me directly: "A lover."

I can't say I was shocked. To be friends with Fats, it helps to be shock proof. The only surprising wrinkle was that Fats had somehow kept Darby out of the press, away from TMZ.

"Congratulations," I said. "I'm happy you found someone. I've seen you on TV walking all those red carpets. Could never tell if those dates were for show, or if you had someone serious. It makes me feel good to know you've got the right partner."

Fats smiled at me.

"We'll be on the ground in a few," she said. "Listen to what I'm saying. Darby is a partner. Not *the* partner. I decided a long time ago it was crazy to limit my pleasure to half the world's population. Just as I don't limit my pleasure to any one person. Too much excitement out there in the world to cut off options."

She could see she had me a little flustered. Not by the notion. But her directness.

"You'll like her," Fats said. "Darby has been asking me to bring around a new friend to join us. Let's see if you make the cut for her."

The pilot broke in on the speaker before I had to decide whether to object. Or not.

"Dr. Pike," he said. "Just received an urgent communication from Chapel Hill. Inspector Pauley asks that you call him immediately upon landing."

Chapter 31

He's the Pope of the porch, where he holds court,
passing judgment every night.
He's the Pope of the porch, where he holds court,
deciding wrong and right.

he plane's satellite internet service was down. No email to check. No cell phone service. It was like waiting through the intermission of a Hitchcock film, on edge, anticipating the next plot development. What urgent news could Pauley have?

As soon as the wheels hit the runway pavement, the cell phone signal kicked in. Fats dialed Pauley and put him on speaker.

"Dr. Pike," he said, when he answered. No small talk to start. "At 12:27 p.m. today, FBI agents responded to a call in an off-campus neighborhood in Chapel Hill and found two adults deceased—one male, one female."

He didn't pause to hear our reactions or questions.

"The official line is that state and local police will proceed with an investigation into a probable murder-suicide, with the husband as the killer and wife as victim."

"Unofficially . . ." This is where he paused.

Fats picked up on the unspoken question.

"Proceed, Inspector," she said. "You have my word that Lassie and I will keep everything you say here in confidence."

"Unofficially," he said, again, "we believe there is a connection to Mallette. The male, Max Whitehall, was adjunct in the statistics department. From initial interviews and even superficial record checks, we can see he had run up enormous gambling debts. Owed more than $1 million—possibly more. That's what we can spot right away, across second and third mortgages, credit cards, bookies, and check kiting. Scene indicates Max shot his wife through the forehead as she slept. Then killed himself. Scene is not fresh. Technicians are pinning down time of death now. My expectation is that this will tie back to Thursday morning, when Mallette was killed."

"So you think . . ." I began.

"I don't think anything," Pauley said. "You never heard any of this. It's unofficial."

He cleared his throat.

"I know you and Dr. Pike were close to Mallette. I want you to know what we know. And what we think we know."

"Thank you, Inspector," I said.

"Female is Dr. Beatriz Martins. Went by Bea. Professor of romance languages. Max had booked a whole lot of the debt in Bea's name, so she was facing a deep pit. Problem for her was that she'd been denied a promotion within her department. Meant she was going to lose out on any chance for tenure. For a faculty member, this was a death sentence. She had exhausted formal appeals and had met with Mallette personally. More than once. As recently as this past Tuesday. He produced a written report of the meeting. Was sympathetic to a frustrated junior faculty member. But he found no reason to override the department chair's decision on the promotion and tenure. Appeal denied."

"And this gives Max motive and opportunity," Fats said. Not a question.

Pauley: "The timeline works. Max knew of Mallette's early morning walks. He was up early on Thursday and found him by Caldwell. Used the knitting needle in the brain—his wife has a hobby room full of art supplies, including knitting needles. Revenge for Mallette refusing his wife the tenure needed to give the family a sinecure. Max then returns to Buttons Road. Shoots his wife. Poses her with her hands crossed over her chest, as if in prayer. Then does himself."

Pauley was ready to wrap up.

"I expect some version of this will hit the press tomorrow. The Bureau wants Mallette solved. Porter wants to reopen Monday. Stay in touch with me directly on the facts. Don't believe what you read," he said. He clicked off.

The steward had the plane's exit door open, the foldout stairs ready. I grabbed my backpack and my leather travel bag. The steward would carry Fats's bag to the black SUV waiting just outside the fence.

Fats was down the steps first. Headed toward the SUV.

Leaning against the SUV was a tall woman. She wore a long leather coat, and I could make out leather pants draped around her ankles.

Her leather boots were worn dull, but still in a deep-purple shade. Black glasses. Auburn hair pulled back in a ponytail.

I waved to say hello. Nothing back.

Fats turned back to me.

"Oh, yeah," she said. "Darby is blind. Don't make an ass of yourself."

Chapter 32

At large in the world, and having good time.
Don't be working too hard, her postcard is signed.
Take care I'll see you my plans aren't too clear.
It's boat rides and treasures, a new world out here.
Hope all is well, her message is signed.
At large in the world, and having good time.

Fats had booked us into two suites in the Four Seasons. Midtown Atlanta. One suite for her and Darby. One for me. I took a shower with jets so strong the spray stung my back.

The ride over had been a hoot.

Learned that Darby is an artist. Works with textiles. Everything from velvet to burlap, she said.

When we loaded our bags into the SUV, Darby first got into the driver's seat and started the car. Actually drove a stretch through the parking lot before she couldn't keep the gag going and laughed out loud. She switched with Fats.

I was enjoying the show but too scared to speak up. If the blind girl is going to drive us to the hotel, let's buckle up and go.

"Holly says she inspired your song about the fair-skinned brunette," Darby said, once she had surrendered the steering wheel. "Any truth to that? Or did our Dr. Pike use that line just to get into my pants?"

This was going to be fun.

"The long ago version of Holly—the young girl I knew as Fats a lifetime ago in Chapel Hill, that was the inspiration for that song," I said. "Today's version, Dr. Pike, billionaire CEO, would require some other kind of tune."

She was too smart to take the bait.

"You joining us for the late-night Panhead show?" Darby asked.

"For absolute certain," I said. "The last 100 hours or so have been more than I can process. I need a night out with those boys. Thank you for letting me tag along."

Fats blew the horn at a Toyota Tundra soaking up space in our lane. Darby flipped the bird—but aimed it in the wrong direction and upset a proper Buckhead mother in her Audi.

"You're gonna be doing more than tagging along," Darby said. She reached back between the seats to swat my knee as she teased me. Missed me entirely and banged the console.

Back at the Four Seasons, the valet frowned. We shrugged.

Called Siler on my personal cell while waking up the laptop and navigating onto the Four Seasons Wi-Fi.

"You hear from Pauley," Siler asked, right off.

"Yeah. Got the official line on Whitehall and off-the-record forecast on the connection to Mallette," I said.

"Cops are all over my place. You thought it was bad before. Now Pig Farm is like a crime scene," he said.

"What?"

"Max Whitehall. Remember, he was my degenerate gambler. Kicked him out of our neighborly $2 pool. The FBI is all up my ass looking at emails and phone calls from the son of a bitch. Talking to my customers. The only smart thing the guy ever did was off himself. We can thank him that there will be no trial."

"Circus still in town?" I asked.

"You know the attention span. Media row has moved away from the old Silent Sam spot and Caldwell monument and over to Whitehall's house. Fancy place on Buttons Road. Neighbors gotta be apoplectic," he said.

Once media made the connection from Whitehall to Mallette, we both concluded, the public appetite for narrative would mostly be fulfilled. As it turned out, the timing lined up nicely with Porter's pledge to reopen the University on Monday. And Fats mentioned, on the plane, he would announce her $100 million gift to create the Mallette Center for Public Service, which would facilitate student service to high-need North Carolina communities.

"See you Monday morning," he said. "I gotta go brew more coffee for these Bureau suits."

Siler clicked off.

My laptop had formulated a relationship with the Four Seasons Wi-Fi.

I had the rest of the afternoon and most of the evening to work.

Fats said we would hook up between 9:00 and 10:00 p.m. for food and then head to Five Paces for the late-night gig. I got a text from Jefferson Hart that he had hitched a ride on the bus with the guys, and he'd do a half-hour to open the set. He asked if it would be okay to open with "Fair-Skinned Brunette". Sure, I told him. An honor.

I crisscrossed through the GRL platforms and signed into the most private portal, reserved for senior executives of the firm—and for me.

After the horror of Mallette's murder, the time with Pearl, and trying to manage Pauley, Porter, and my own feelings, I had to spend a few minutes brushing up on my own methodology. I had programmed multiple GRL databases, plus some outside security systems, to put checkmarks beside the names of 118,223 associates. Every individual would receive a score, ranging from 0 to 5.

A score of 5 would mean the individual received checkmarks for every one of the following variables:

- Authors whose publications had swung quickly from mediocre content (or rejected content) to newsworthy articles

- Employees who had been passed over for a promotion recently or received a big promotion

- Employees who recently were linked to litigation

- Employees with big swings in personal finances

- Employees with recent real estate transactions

I was back on track. This is all about needles. Not haystacks.

The analysis I had initiated on Friday night had run without interruption. The output was stored in a file on my GRL desktop—essentially a folder in the cloud with an accompanying visual to give users the faux confidence that whatever they were clicking was actually on their computer.

In the output file were names of thirty-seven individuals with a score of 5.

Chapter 33

I attend the daily service, at a special house of worship,
where the congregation looks up at the sky.

Get on my knees and say, Father bless me on this day,
forgive my sins and help me make the try.

The first variable in my list was the big deal. Without this condition, I would have had thousands of names in the output. But in the world of academic publishing, status quo rules. Authors don't shoot to the front like teenage singers on the pop charts. There aren't many supernovas.

Seventeen of the names were faculty members at prestigious universities around the world; the other twenty were GRL researchers working in GRL labs. Of these, five were based in the Tokyo lab, eight in Budapest, two in Lima, three in New York, and two in Atlanta. None in Cape Town.

The second of my variables carried implications in both directions. Some of these associates had been passed over for promotion recently. Others had received a big promotion.

I sorted the list of thirty-seven by this question.

Ten of the names made my list because things had taken a bad turn. They had been passed over for promotion. These could be people with an axe to grind against GRL. They could be whistleblowers. Or they could be making up accusations to throw dirt. Anger and spite are terrific motivators.

The remaining twenty-seven individuals were supernovas—shooting stars, in every way. Everything was rolling for these people. If you believe in the "if it's too good to be true" admonition, these are the individuals to suspect of cooking the numbers. What else would explain a sudden turnaround and explosion of success?

I ordered Four Seasons room service and kept grinding through the data. The most extraordinary fruit plate arrived, with a cream cheese dipping sauce and hot banana bread. I drank hot tea and dipped berries into the goo.

It was fun searching for the needle.

I sorted by the litigation variable next. I was curious as to what kind of engagement all these folks would have with a court system. It turns out there was plenty of opportunity.

Most of the legal issues had to do with intellectual property. Some scientists had recently filed for patents. Some had sued over patents. Or been sued over patents. One scientist in the Lima lab was tangled in a child-custody and divorce case. The most exotic legal connection came via the SEC. A researcher from a Texas university, who previously worked in the Budapest lab, was currently accused of insider trading, essentially using proprietary research data—prior to journal publication—to make trades in Big Pharma stocks. Some of his former Budapest colleagues were drawn into the case, which explained the outside representation from that lab.

The surprise came from the Tokyo office. GRL researcher Rin Itou had burst into superstardom in the last three years. With advanced degrees in engineering and biology, Rin had moved from a post-doc fellowship into a prominent research role at GRL right away. But over the next decade or so, she settled into routine publishing in the second-tier journals. Never a failure. But never a star. She was the definition of a "consistent." Plenty of researchers spend their career at that level, so no surprise. They are part of great teams, but they are never the brand-name scientist leading a breakthrough. Being part of the scientific machinery is enough for most people. Or it's all they have in them.

Then, three years ago, Rin's work became electric. She began publishing articles about the potential for using biologics to program cells—human cells—to carry out behaviors that we want them to do at the precise time we want. If we want a cell to fight cancer, we push a button on our iPhone to tell it do so. If we want a cell to burn insulin differently, the same remote control functions work. By implication, if we want to have bright green eyes, we can tell our cells to make that happen, also. Rin was a curiosity when her early studies reported on simulations in what amounted to high-end Petri dishes. It was one thing to program one or two rat cells. It would be another thing to manage our cellular, biologic behavior the way we manage our iTunes. But that's pretty much the sound bite she uttered on CNN International that made her a supernova.

"If you can pick a song on your phone, you can tell your cells what to do," she said to the anchor. It was all over YouTube. "With these SyNaptz advancements, we'll put technology into your hands that enables you to manage your health to better outcomes."

Within a year, mainstream news outlets were covering every new item she published in the scientific journals. CNN International covered her work, and NPR embedded a reporter in her lab as part of a feature on women leaders in scientific fields.

GRL promoted Rin to run the Tokyo lab. That brought a big bump in pay. And Rin had structured her deal to share in the royalties from the patented biologics and cellular inventions. Rin bought houses in Tokyo and New York.

Then, the legal stuff. That was the surprise.

Rin was killed in a car accident back in March. Her death occurred during a year when Tokyo was posting a record number of traffic fatalities. Rin was, in the end, rendered a statistic. The GRL empire moved on. The Tokyo lab had new leadership. Fats was on her way to her next billion. The biologics and SyNaptz were unstoppable.

It was 9:00 p.m.

The hotel extension rang twice. Stopped before I could get across the room to pick up the handset.

My GRL cell phone buzzed.

"Hey, Fats. You ready?" I said.

It was Darby's voice.

"Cashmere, angora, or silk?"

"All of the above," I said, and clicked off.

A few minutes later, a knock on the door.

It was Darby. Wearing gold leather pants, cashmere sweater, silk scarf wrapped around her head. Black leather boots. Black sunglasses.

"What? No angora?" I asked.

She bobbed her head, and I saw dangling earrings swing back and forth from either ear. Gold baubles were hung on tightly-wound fibers. Angora, no doubt.

She hooked her arm, inviting me to loop my hand inside.

Chapter 34

God and country and casserole.
Hand-turned freezers and sausage balls.

Persimmon pudding and Cheerwine cake.
Seven-layer salad and Shake n Bake.

From the ladies of First Baptist Church,
we got Crisco religion and tough love first.

*S*aturday night in October. Empire State South in Atlanta. 9:51 p.m.

We ordered nearly everything on Hugh Acheson's menu. Pickled vegetables. Cured meats. Pimento cheese topped with bacon marmalade.

Rye whiskey for me. Bottle of Stuhlmuller cab for Fats and Darby. Or two bottles. Who knows.

The weather held up, and we played bocce in the cold courtyard and drank and told lies and forgot about Mallette and GRL and everything. Darby was the bocce winner. Don't ask me how.

Darby and Fats met five years ago, at Art Basel in Miami.

Fats was immediately attracted to her, which I could see. Everyone in the restaurant was attracted to Darby. When she touched my arm, I felt the heat of her skin. She must have felt me flinch.

"I run hot," she said.

The two women fell into what Darby described as full-time, part-time relationship. Together several weeks a year. One or two international trips a year.

Darby had an art studio, and Fats had helped her open a gallery in the Highlands—an investment that gave Fats a nice financial return, Darby explained.

Darby produced and sold all kinds of textiles—jewelry, clothes, rugs, and other objects. She swiped through pics on her phone, showing me items for sale in her gallery. I don't know how she worked the phone and didn't ask.

"I fell for her when she turned out to be the only person who didn't care about my day job," Fats said. "I told her, once, that I was developing new technology that we could use to program her cells, to make her eyes work."

"And I told her to go fuck herself," Darby said.

"I told her nobody talks to billionaires that way," Fats said.

"And I told her I couldn't see the dollar signs," Darby responded.

She poured more wine.

"She did say that," Fats said. She touched her knee.

"The world I see is beautiful," Darby said. "The world you see—from what cable news tells me—is ugly. I'm good with sound, smell, touch, and taste. So many of you are handicapped by your sight. You can't imagine things beyond that which enters your field of vision. I'm enabled by an ability to see whatever I can imagine."

I sipped my whiskey.

"Holly says you were minutes away from walking her down the aisle," Darby continued. "A long time ago."

"A long time ago," I repeated.

"A long, long time ago," Fats said.

"Ever construct an alternate history? Figure out how the world would have spun differently if you two had married?" Darby asked me.

"Yes," I said. Let it go at that.

The waiter cleared the table. Darby had asked a yes-or-no question and let the answer sit there, untouched. I wasn't going to help her any.

"Nearly showtime, guys," Fats said, settling up the check. "Let's get over to Five Paces for some music."

Walking to the black SUV, holding up traffic on 10th Street, Fats and Darby holding hands. The roles were different now, but the vibe was just like freshman year. Pretty people and late nights and live music. Choosing to see what we wanted to see. Choosing to believe anything was possible. Darby, nearly a head taller than her lover, pinched Fats on her ass as she climbed into the truck. I closed the door behind them both and jumped into the back seat.

Fats dialed up Hayes's music on her phone, and we rode to the show listening to him sing about the girl who left him for Jesus.

I could sympathize.

Chapter 35

I fell in love with Emmylou.
I don't know what to do.
Can't tell my wife, cannot tell a lie.
I don't know what to do.

*F*ive Paces is a neighborhood bar that reached its optimal state in about 1961. Or maybe 1966. Or maybe even 1973. No matter. It hit the pause button sometime in there and became a living relic. There was smoke. There were no appetizers. There were chick bartenders who could toss a drunk out on his ass. There were no hostesses. The bar was wood. The floor concrete. The stuffing bursting from beneath the leather in the booths.

The jukebox was aggressively programmed with old rock and roll, blues, and roots country music. Everything from Willie Dixon to Donnie Fritts. The place is what we all hoped Pig Farm could become in another half-century.

The owner—a guy introduced to me only as Uno—had no left arm. The sleeve on his jean jacket was cut off and sewn over at the shoulder.

Darby and Fats, no surprise, were semi-regulars here. Uno had a guy manning an orange cone out front, and we pulled the SUV into a parking space six feet from the door. The top half of the door was glass. The bottom half plywood. I could hear guitars tuning.

It was an intimate show. About 100 people in the room. Jefferson kicked things off and did a series of tunes he and I had written. Started with "Fair-Skinned Brunette". Then did an amazing job with "Brownsville Tonight." He had a horn player tonight, and it made the song.

He came back with "The Displaced Man" and sang in such a mournful voice that it pulled in the whole room. Not one person was speaking.

I dreamed of San Francisco but wound up in Millbrae.
I used to want a book deal, but now there's nothing left to say.

I've mostly made my peace, don't wonder too much why.
But I still dream of Gimghoul Road, and the Pilgrim's Progress makes me cry.

Green tea and green label,
keep my mind alert, my liver stable.
Doing less than I am able.
I've become The Displaced Man.
I've become The Displaced Man.

Jeff wrapped up the set of our songs with "She's a Bad Decision," which turned things back up in the room. Darby pulled me out on the dance floor. In her boots, she was an inch taller than I was. I could see the angora in her earrings as she pressed into me. Her leather pants slid off my jeans. Jeff's electric guitar was roaring. Uno was pouring Kamikaze shooters up and down the bar.

She wears blood diamonds and real mink.
She takes tips off the table and doesn't blink.

No tan lines, no panties there.
She knows you know and doesn't care.
She sips Chartreuse and holds your stare.
She twists her finger through her hair.

Jefferson had made me look good, and I bought a round of whiskey for him and the band. He wrapped up his set with three new songs from his CD. His new bride was with him, and she swung her hips back and forth, standing on the side of the stage, watching her man perform. The last tune had a great mandolin part, and Jeff was spectacular.

Fats was leaning against Darby, who was leaning against the bar. They looked like movie stars together. Bulletproof and creative, moving through the world, knowing there was no barrier that could stop them from pursuing pleasure.

My personal cell phone buzzed. Fished it out of my leather jacket. Text from Siler.

"News breaking in the early editions of Sunday's paper. 'Officials close to investigation point to Whitehall as Mallette's killer.' Good that you're missing the circus."

No need to reply.

Uno poured me a new whiskey.

LTD and Panhead came out together, like a songwriter night at the Bluebird. Told stories. Told lies. Sang their own songs, in turn, and sang one another's songs. Plugged their gig tomorrow night at Terminal West.

Then, I heard LTD call me out.

"Since we're making this a Lassie James festival tonight, let me play you a new one Lassie wrote for one of those Teen Idol singers," he said, drawing a huge laugh from Panhead and Jeff.

He moved into an electrified version of "Snow Day," having improved the structure of the song and added some punch to the lyrics. And got a good response from the crowd.

"Not his best work," Panhead said, "but maybe it's passable for 2:00 a.m. in Georgia. Can't imagine it'll fly in New Braunfels."

The boys played until late turned into early, until Uno said he had to leave to get ready for church, until Darby and Fats and I had danced with each other too many times to figure out who was dancing with whom.

"Waffle House," Fats said, when Uno pulled away in his Camaro, silver crucifix dangling from his rearview mirror.

We left the SUV parked and climbed into the black car Fats had summoned. Good to be a billionaire.

"Waffle House," Darby said, endorsing the choice.

She turned to me: "And then you will join us in our bed."

Chapter 36

Surfed with Linda Ronstadt. Cooked for Raquel Welch.
Tattoos never turn out right, and memories just melt.

I didn't eat much. What to order before a threesome? A new one on me. Poked at cheese grits and drank a gallon of hot tea.

Darby made a show of reading the menu closely. Then inhaled a plate of hash browns loaded with everything in the store. Fats stuck with a veggie omelet. She left the waitress a $100 tip.

Back at the Four Seasons, true to her word, Darby invited me into their suite.

It was a hotel suite like none I'd ever seen. I perceived Darby was in charge. Or maybe wished it. Either way, she pulled me toward the bathroom, which was larger than my living room back in Chapel Hill. Fats hung back.

The shower was enormous. Shower heads mounted in the ceiling and the walls. All the walls. She turned on all the handles. Water and steam were filling the space.

Darby said she wanted to watch me undress. Crossed her arms like she meant it. I complied. Got into the shower, hot spray hitting me from this side and that side.

Through the foggy glass, I watched Darby fling her boots against the wall. Wriggle out of the gold leather pants. Toss away the cashmere and scarf like crepe paper.

She found the handle of the shower door and joined me in the room. We let the soaking take effect. Washing away smoke from Five Paces and grease from Waffle House and grit from the bocce court.

Fats came in, wrapped in a Four Seasons robe. Dropped the robe to the floor and stood under the spray with us.

There was soap and foam and steam and laughter.

The only words came from Darby.

"Did she tell you?" Darby asked me, as she rubbed shampoo into her hair.

Fats had washed my back. I was now returning the favor. I said nothing.

"I had asked Holly to bring a third into our bed. I really did," Darby said, water streaming into her hair and rinsing the soap down her face and over her shoulders.

"But I wanted another girl. When she told me she was bringing a guy—bringing you, I cried," Darby said. "It was like I asked her for cobbler, and she served me pie."

Fats nodded to me, confirming the story.

We all rinsed. Darby turned off one handle. Then another. Then, all the spray stopped.

Fats stepped back into her robe. Handed a robe to Darby. Another one to me. I was dizzy from whiskey, grits, steam, and a lot of skin against skin.

"Then when I danced with you tonight, I changed my mind. You have good texture. You have many good textures. I could feel the rough and the smooth, the cold side of the silk in your heart and the barbed wire of your temper."

Fats opened the door and headed toward the bed. It had been turned down. By a professional. Plates of chocolate-covered strawberries were on nightstands on both sides of the bed. Somebody—Fats, I guess—had the Beatles running through speakers, hidden somewhere.

Darby sat on the side of the bed, her legs hanging off. She patted the spot beside her. Waved toward me.

I sat down beside her.

She put her mouth by my right ear. Whispered.

"One last thing," she said, in the quietest breath.

She reached into the nightstand drawer. Pulled out two cashmere wraps. Handmade, customized sleep masks. Something like the Lone Ranger might wear, but with a better fit and no eyeholes.

Darby tossed one on the bed. Fats dropped the robe. Got into bed. Placed the cashmere over her eyes.

Darby placed the cashmere apparel over my eyes. The world went dark.

"Now there," she said. "We're all working from the same senses."

Darby pulled her feet into the bed, and me with her.

She put her lips to my ear again. Bit my earlobe and said, "Is it true you're writing a song about a woman who's a Baptist and a Communist?"

Chapter 37

Rich man counts his dollar bills, the wealthy counts his time.
Rich man holds his cash for thrills, smart man tracks the chimes.

I don't know what happened in that great big bed. I couldn't see a thing.

Chapter 38

Saturday night is for pickin'.
Sunday the preacher stops by.
Monday is for shelling peas.
Tuesday cards and dice.

Wednesday brings the Garden Club.
Thursday the sheriff drops in.
Friday is for cooking liquor.
Then tune the mandolin.

*S*unday afternoon in October. Four Seasons suite. 7:03 p.m.

I snuck away from the bed of blind love sometime after the noon hour, when I found a moment. I was awake, and the angels were dreaming. Might as well take a lesson from Mallette and use the moment.

I ghosted, really. Didn't say a word. Crawled from the bed until I pawed my way to the bathroom. Pulled my clothes into a pile. Put on a robe. Made my way back to the suite's living room and allowed a half-hour for my eyes to adjust.

Walked down the hall to my own suite and slept until 6:30 p.m.

Dreamed of touches and sensations I had never known before. Of physical pleasure emanating from deep inside me, not from outside stimuli. Dreamed of rough, wet burlap sacks filled with old oyster shells, lined around a fire pit at Emerald Isle. The smell of burgers on a grate over the flames. The grit of sand on the beach towel, and the softness of lips kissing my neck. The beach was dark, and the fire added no real light, and I dreamed of how the wind blew salt into my hair and carried sound from the house beyond the dune. I dreamed of my muscles aching and how the strings from a bikini worn by a pretty girl touched my cheek as she sat in my lap. I grabbed the string in my teeth and pulled. The kite was back in my dreams, breaking away from its owner and flying into the sky, illuminated as if by flame. Sand crabs ran from the surf. Lightning struck the ground around me.

The hotel phone rang.

It was Fats.

"I need you drinking plenty of liquids," she said. No preamble. "Play part of the weekend is done. Now some work time. Meet me in my suite in thirty."

She hung up.

I fell back into my sleep, and into the dream. I dreamed of my blind hand brushing over skin. There was soft skin and shivering skin and skin rough with stubble. Wet places and dry places. Long hair smelling of oatmeal soap in my face, and the feel of a calf muscle tightening in my hand as my partner slipped into climax. Notes from a thousand bowed psalteries filled the beach, overwhelming the noise of the tides, as we floated above the sand, looking down on the fire below us and up into the sky lit up by rogue kites on fire against the stars. I could feel the tension of the bikini string in my teeth, the salty mist from the surf aggravating my eyes. The psaltery notes grew louder, the cry of mountain strings quivering against the spruce soundboards. The burning gasses from the sun rising in the

East, over the ocean's horizon, brought instant silence to the beach. I woke up suddenly. An hour late to see Fats, but replenished in a way I had never felt. As if a seraph had chased the devil from my soul.

Fats answered the door in all black—jeans, sweater, and hairband.

She swung open the door to the big suite, turned her back to me, and returned to the seat at her desk. She had two iPhones on the desk and a laptop humming.

"What do you have on Bootstrap?" she asked.

She sensed me pausing to check the suite.

"Darby is back at her studio," she said. "Sends her love. And a small gift."

Fats handed me a small flat package wrapped with braids of cotton and wool. I stuck it in my backpack.

I briefed Fats on my analysis and the report I had reviewed yesterday. Took an easy chair near her desk and opened my laptop. Described the output files and delivered highlights to Fats on the thirty-seven individuals who emerged with a score of 5. Described the university faculty in the pool and the individuals based at GRL labs. Fats looked twice at her watch.

I talked faster.

The Budapest lab, I explained, had all kinds of problems, telling her something she may or may not have already known. She gave no clue. Covered the tragic story of Rin, assuming she must have personal knowledge of the loss of a supernova researcher but hoping my data would be useful.

"Budapest," she said, when I paused. "I've been tracking the SEC case against the senior researcher we had there. A lone rogue, I was told, and now he's gone. In fact, all of the internal reports have claimed the Budapest lab is beyond suspicion. You have new information here on the number of potential risks in that lab. Eight red flags is an eight-alarm fire."

Fats asked me to pull every published article and every rejected journal submission from the past five years from all eight Budapest associates identified through my analysis. We would set up an independent review committee to put fresh eyes on the material and a data team to rerun all the analyses. GRL needed to see if the analyses were replicable.

"I'm on it," I said. "Or will be after this bloody dissertation defense tomorrow."

"Yes, Dr. Battle," Fats said, smiling and bowing in mock deference. "You'll knock 'em dead. And I expect you'll be off to Budapest soon. We'll get you a table at Costes."

"Just send the GRL jet for me," I said, half kidding, but not really. A coach seat to Budapest held no appeal, no matter the million-dollar consulting fee.

Fats closed her laptop and turned toward me.

"Flying on the GRL jet could become a regular gig," she said. "You're as good as Mallette said. You really can find needles in a haystack."

Chapter 39

She asked for cobbler. I brought pie.
The day I made a blind girl cry.
She did not give a reason why.
Just told me that our love had died.
We never did see eye to eye.
She was bold. I was shy.
I could not look at her and lie.
Some days I really did not try.
My gut was tight, my mouth went dry.
She cursed at me and said goodbye.
Cold hard truth, I could not deny.
I think I'm going to blame the pie.
The day I made a blind girl cry.

onday morning in October. Thirty-thousand feet in the air. Somewhere between Atlanta and Chapel Hill. 5:43 a.m.

It was Monday morning for me but still late Sunday night for Siler and Jefferson.

Fats was in the CEO seat on the jet.

I was in a big leather seat pouring caffeinated tea into my body. I had been up most of the night playing with a song about Darby. The GRL satellite Wi-Fi connection was up and running this time, so I was able to shoot the lyrics to Siler and Jefferson. They were bouncing through the last quarter-mile of a late-night adventure and found the song brilliant. Siler emailed that Jeff had pulled out the banjo and was already playing around with a driving bluegrass riff. He imagined an *a cappella* cold opening to the song, then a banjo kicking like marbles banging through a tumble dry cycle.

Emails came in from Porter, also. There was a lot of stagecraft set up for the afternoon, and he had had to play around with the schedule to suit the VIPs who wanted to be on hand for the reopening of the University. This was being compared to the reopening of the University after the Civil War. The circus was back on Franklin Street, he said.

The ceremonies would begin at 1:00 p.m. Scratched plans for Memorial Hall. Defense would be in Gerrard, as planned. Porter would announce three things.

First, this ceremony would mark the reopening of the University, with academic departments resuming a full schedule and all student activities and athletic events back on.

Second, Porter would announce that Mallette's public memorial service would be held November 1 in the Smith Center.

Third, he would announce the $100 million gift from Fats to create the Sanders Arthel Mallette Center for Public Service. The new center would facilitate opportunities for every undergraduate to deliver public service in high-need North Carolina communities.

With CNN and CSPAN planning to air all of this live, the Gerrard Hall event had become a tough ticket. University presidents from across the country had flown into Chapel Hill to provide a symbolic and literal show of support for the freedoms associated with an open campus. Until the FBI found the Max Whitehall connection, these presidents had federal guards in their office. Mallette's murder revealed the national security issues in the offices of university presidents, and Mallette's peers wanted to show up to honor his memory.

So, presidents from the top of US News & World Report rankings would be on the first few rows of my defense. The president would be there, also. Among other things, she would name Fats as White House Science Advisor. Then, whichever tenured faculty had been invited by Porter would be in the room.

My only feedback was that it would be nice to have some actual students in the room. Seemed gauche to announce the new center for public service without allowing any real students in the room. Porter agreed and said he would work it out.

Once he had completed these announcements, he would invite the four remaining members of my committee to the stage. A fifth chair, Mallette's, would be empty. Porter would call me to the stage and provide a brief explanation of how the doctoral defense would unfold. Members would have ninety minutes to ask questions of me about my dissertation—or about anything, really. Then, committee members would retire to an anteroom to vote. Upon their return, members voting in favor would sign the cover page of my dissertation. I had sent Rose Bynum, Mallette's assistant, the electronic document. She had the signing page printed and ready. In theory, it took three member signatures to secure an approved dissertation. Taken with other requirements already satisfied, this would secure, for me, the degree of doctor of philosophy—or PhD. It was ritual theater, usually carried out in solitude. Today, it felt like being in East Germany the day after the wall came down in 1989. In practice, nearly every defense ended with all five members signing the cover page. If a doctoral student had a serious problem with one or more members, it meant he or she would likely never get to a defense scheduled. Hence, the great number of students carrying the "ABD" title around their necks—signifying their status as "all but dissertation." They might as well have never entered grad school.

I cleaned up the email exchanges with Porter.

We were near RDU, where, no doubt, Fats's Coulee would be waiting.

I got an email from Rose.

"When you land at the private aviation place, I'll be there to pick you up. Pearl came back late last night and needs to see you right away. I'll drive you back to campus so you can meet with her first thing," Rose said in her email.

I closed the laptop and shut my eyes, until I heard the wheels scrape the runway. I could see Pearl looking through my eyes, like Grace Kelly clocking Jimmy Stewart.

Chapter 40

I haven't lost Alicia yet, but I'm afraid the end is near.
I haven't reached the edge of the earth, but I believe I can see it from here.
I believe I can see it from here.

ats hopped in the Coulee, shouting "Break a leg, Dr. Battle." The steward put her bags in the big trunk. Rose was there, as promised, and I got in the car with her. She was pale from days without much sleep, but she had a spark back in her eyes. She hugged me when I got to the car.

"Dr. Mallette would be so proud of you," she said, her voice breaking partway through the quick line.

She kept to the right lane on the freeway back to Chapel Hill.

"It was so horrible about Professor Bea," she continued. "The students loved her. She was one of my favorites, too. And stuck married to that . . . monster."

"So you were in the office this week when she met with Mallette?" I asked. I was wishing for a biscuit but didn't want to ask Rose to go out of her way.

"Yes, I was there. FBI have been all over me about that meeting. They're desperate to find that package," she said. "Turning his private residence upside down. His University house, also. And the office. And Dr. Pike's security people are right there with the FBI agents. Quail Hill is a mess"

"What package?"

"What Bea left for him. Don't know what was in it. No one knows. But the FBI agents sure want to know," she said.

"Back up, Rose," I said, bringing my attention back from the biscuits to the information she had to share. "I thought the meeting was about her promotion? About her appeal on tenure."

"Yes, she had met with Dr. Mallette about that a bunch lately. She had a lot of complaints about the languages department. She couldn't catch a break," she said.

"Rose, you were with Mallette how long?" I asked.

"Twenty years."

"And you heard a lot, learned a lot, saw a lot?" I asked.

"Sure. I heard everything. Arguments. Funny stories. Sad stories," she said.

My mind was fully focused on Rose now.

"Let's back up even more," I said. "Tell me about Bea and Dr. Mallette."

Rose explained that Bea had begun seeking advice from Mallette more than a year ago, before he was selected as chancellor. His ability to navigate university politics made him the first choice for mentor among many faculty members. He apparently had a fondness for Bea.

She consistently won teaching awards but was never promoted. For the first decade or so of her career, it turned out, she was more or less a lecturer. She taught introductory courses in Portuguese to freshmen and sophomores. She made her real money doing sophisticated translation jobs for university clients, publishers, the government, and private clients.

"She was gifted with languages. A kind of genius really," Rose continued. "She was teaching these intro Portuguese classes, but she could work in Arabic, Russian, Japanese, French, Portuguese, Spanish. And English, of course."

The courts needed something translated, Bea became the go-to expert. Then, she was hired on to military jobs, some public and some secret. The big museums around the world loved her. She told all kinds of stories about being at exhibit openings in Cairo and Lisbon and St. Petersburg. Then, Big Pharma started calling. Somebody has to figure out how to explain Viagra to a global population.

"Bea could translate anything from a medical pamphlet to a set of IKEA directions," she said, laughing. "I remember Dr. Mallette calling her, once, when he was invited to give a talk in Tokyo. She made sure he arrived at the conference with English and Japanese versions of his paper."

"So what happened Tuesday?" I asked.

"You sound like the FBI," she said. It made her face sag to say the letters. "Tuesday was actually a good meeting. Or seemed like it."

Bea had exhausted the department appeals. She had been hired fourteen years ago as an assistant professor and was still an assistant professor and wasn't going to get promoted. Her department chair was an asshole.

"He told her: 'You want to teach kids new languages, go work for Rosetta Stone,'" Rose relayed to me.

The University, no surprise, wanted scholarship. It didn't want a faculty member who could help a kid learn to speak Portuguese—or to get excited about how a new language could open doors. The University wanted faculty writing books about Portuguese literature or Russian economics or something. Mallette found the department chair a bore but couldn't argue the position on the merits.

Mallette believed Bea was simply a fish out of water. Pursuing tenure was a dead end for her because she wasn't a researcher at heart. Mallette had been looking for a new and better fit for her. On Tuesday, Rose explained, Mallette presented Bea with a new idea: he proposed naming her executive director of a new campus center promoting year-abroad programs for undergraduates. She would continue to teach language classes, while also organizing year-abroad programs for undergraduates from across campus.

"She had to do something," Rose said. "The online stuff was ruining her translation business."

Made sense. If cars no longer needed drivers, translation services would no longer need translators. More and more, translation clients were relying on Google and similar platforms to do the work Bea used to do.

"She actually seemed relieved to hear about the new position Mallette had found for her," Rose said. "They hugged."

"And the package?" I asked.

"When they came out of his office, they hugged standing by my desk. And she reached into her bag and handed him a brown envelope. More of a package, really. We see so much paper on this campus. And this had a lot of paper stuffed in it. Boy, the FBI really hit me hard on this."

I let her catch her breath.

"Then Dr. Mallette handed the package to me and walked her to the door. I put the package with his daily mail."

"What happened to that mail?" I asked.

"I know it was in his leather bag when he left Tuesday evening," she said. "From there, who knows?"

Maybe he threw it away. Maybe it was under magazines in his bathroom. Or in his University residence.

"He's been so busy, and everybody has an idea to share with him about the next big thing. They all want him to back them. He had so many things pushed into his hands. I don't know if he ever even read half of them," Rose said.

We were pulling into the Carolina Inn parking lot.

"Pearl will meet you here," Rose said. "In the lobby."

I was rushing now.

"Rose, what did Bea say to Mallette about the envelope? About the package?" I asked.

"Not a lot. Just that the package contained a kind of a puzzle. Something she'd been struggling with. Not sure how to handle—or something like that. The idea of a new job seemed a relief, a load off her shoulders. And it was like giving him the envelope was part of starting over," Rose said.

Pearl was on the porch, waving for me to come into the lobby.

Chapter 41

There's family waiting there,
Keeping warm an extra chair.
And a plate of Dixie food and friends who smile.
God bless the Old North State.
Keep the land and people great.
The trip is always worth the many miles.

*P*earl looked more rested and together than I expected. She wore a long denim skirt. A cotton cable sweater with a V-neck.

We took opposing sofa chairs in the Carolina Inn lobby. When she sat and crossed her legs, I saw weathered tan boots up to her knee.

Seeing her energy made me realize how tired I was—and how god-awful tired and worn out I must look. If I could just get through this defense at 1:00.

"How was Maine?" I asked. "I know it was a crazy turnaround."

"Fine, fine. Most of Dad's personal files are in our Friendly Lane residence here. And the FBI still has that secured as a crime scene. I can't get near it. There were just a few files to go through in Maine. And a copy of his will was there. The Friendly Lane house goes to me," she said.

Her voice broke when she said it. Still impossible to process that her dad wouldn't be there with her in the house.

"Rose said you wanted to see me," I said, picking up the conversation.

"Yeah, yeah." She reached into her bag.

Pearl pulled out her wallet. Poked her fingers into one of the pockets and came out with a small brown metal key, with a square end. A frayed snip of Carolina ribbon tied through a small hole on the key's handle.

"One of the things Dad had stored in Maine was a box from 1984, after he received his second Pulitzer. There are a bunch of letters in there from VIP types sending congratulations—a lot of people apparently hated the Texas judicial system. Chief Justice Burger sent a note! We're donating his papers to the Southern Historical Collection, but I want you to go through those letters with me first. I'd like you to have any that you'd like to frame and keep. I know Dad would want that. And I want you to have his bowties. They should be with you."

"I'm sure it's better to keep all those together with the donated papers," I said, not sure where she was headed with this.

"The box included some family records and legal documentation for the Maine real estate – Mom and Dad's wedding license, my birth certificate, and so on. Even found my baby book in there. It's a hoot."

I couldn't help but smile at the way she lit up the room. She saw me eyeing the key in her hand.

"And then this," she said, holding up the key.

"We don't use keys at the Maine house. I know the Friendly Lane house inside and out, and this key doesn't fit anything there. Can't be anything about his new chancellor position. This box hasn't been touched in ages. What do you think?" she asked.

The disinterest must have been clear in my face. We all pile up keys and toss them into attics. Could be a YMCA locker or an old Woolen Gym basket. Could be to a kid's bike. I didn't know and, in all honesty, didn't care.

"Listen, Pearl," I said, trying to make a show of support. "I know the last few days have been beyond painful. I'm just not sure what answers you'll find in a key."

"I don't, either," she said. "But I don't like loose ends. No genealogist likes loose ends. I thought you'd be willing to help me on this."

"Let me see the key," I said, putting my hand out.

I held it and squeezed it and looked at the crooks and grooves—looked at the years of tarnish.The blue ribbon looped through the hole allowed the key to be hung on a hook or placed on a ring. I thought about my own boxes and storage bins and all the old keys strewn about. Imagined my death and whether anyone would try to solve a riddle about an orphaned key. I thought about my own keys.

What secrets would my keys reveal about me?

Then, Pearl's good energy took hold inside me.

"Pearl, this isn't a loose end at all," I said.

I was up from my chair.

I kissed her. Two short kisses on the lips.

Chapter 42

A school kid took my picture, now it hangs in a museum.
The people stop and shake their heads. I stare back like I see 'em.

I understand Professor Seagull. I shook Joe Mitchell's hand.
The girl I loved, I never told her. Now I never can.

I had Pearl's right hand wrapped up in my left hand, and we were out the door of the Inn onto Columbia Street, through the alleyway beside Carroll Hall and through Polk Place. Past the grand old entrance to Wilson Library.

"I should have worn a hat," she said, her blonde hair blowing this way and that.

"We're close," I said.

Davis Library opened at 8:00 a.m., and we were among the first through the door. I had to speak to two librarians to get to the right administrator. It was a woman named Annemarie, a tattooed, pierced librarian in charge of faculty and graduate student studies.

I introduced myself. More important, I introduced Pearl, explaining to Annemarie that Dr. Mallette's daughter had flown in to handle some family business. Then, I took a chance.

"Annemarie, we have Dr. Mallette's key to his carrel," I said. "The study space was assigned to him many years ago, and I haven't visited him in here in a long time. Can you check the assignments and confirm the location?"

I heard Pearl catch her breath.

Annemarie did what librarians do. She said nothing and put her head down. First, she typed on the keyboard and scanned virtual records. Then, she went through a door in the back and was gone for several minutes. She came back with a scuffed tin box that contained a brick of notecards. Nothing virtual about old-school records. She flipped through the alphabet. Stopping in the obvious places.

Then, she spoke.

"I used to see him in here all the time," she said. "He would hide in the stacks, I believe, to get some time to himself. But there's no record that he has any carrel."

Annemarie reached over and touched Pearl's hand.

"I'm sorry for your loss. He's the only person I've ever seen around here who was irreplaceable," Annemarie said.

"You said he would steal away some private time here in the library?" I asked.

"Yes," Annemarie said. "Pretty common. Faculty are fair game in their offices—office hours, and all. This place is big enough to get lost."

"Can you check another name?" I asked.

Pearl looked at me.

"Sure," Annemarie said. She assumed the typing position at the keyboard.

"I expect this may be an old one, so maybe better off starting with the notecards," I said. "Try the name Doc Watson."

Chapter 43

So swallow the truth.
Look straight in his eyes.
Whisper a prayer,
and tell him sweet lies

All dogs go to heaven.
Reindeer fly through the sky.
The tooth fairy is rich.
Please tell me sweet lies.

allette's carrel was in a corner, on the fourth floor of the 400,000 square-foot building. Annemarie said blue note-cards in the tin box meant the carrel was assigned to a VIP. She had heard that lots of blue cards were assigned as part of the library's grand opening in 1984. Annemarie pointed out that she was born in 1987, as if to provide an alibi for her intial blue card failure. The library opened at a time when Mallette was winning his second Pulitzer and was the biggest name on campus—and before Rose became his assistant. Over time, as the carrel spaces filled up, grad students had to share carrels. Assignments identified with a blue notecard were left alone. Untouchables.

Like everything else, Mallette's carrel was interesting. And neat. On the worktable were three stacks of documents.

On the left were journals and periodicals to be read. These were crisp and not yet creased. On the right were articles and journal issues Mallette had read and annotated. These had page corners turned down, flames of yellow highlight marked through, yellow stickies protruding from the edges. In the trashcan were periodicals that had been read but didn't merit annotations. Those Mallette had marked up would be transferred back to Rose, and she would enter appropriate notations in the annotated bibliography Mallette maintained. It enabled him to retrieve, on demand, critical information on just about any relevant piece of scholarship or journalism he had encountered. We were getting a look inside the assembly line of the factory.

The middle stack included the mail Rose sent home with him. We were looking at the items Rose had sent home with Mallette the last few days of his life. His secret was that he didn't take the mail home. Or to the chancellor's residence. He would steal away time in the carrel to open, review, and trash or retain documents. Anything that needed to be filed, or required a response, was put in the right-hand stack. Every so often, we concluded, he would take that stack back to Rose.

This morning, the middle stack was anchored by a package that seemed to be bursting with papers. Just like Pearl said.

"We should call Pauley," Pearl said. "I don't think he knows about this carrel."

She crossed her arms. She uncrossed her arms. She crossed her arms.

"He doesn't know about it," I said. "Six billion people on the planet, and nobody but you and I know about it. And we're not calling Pauley.

We're not calling anybody. Your dad didn't even tell Rose about it!"

"He's going to be pissed," she said.

"Remember, Pauley leaked everything to *The New York Times* today about Max Whitehall," I said. "When the *Times* says 'federal officials close to the investigation,' that's code for Pauley. And Pauley has solved your dad's murder. That's all he cared about. He'll probably get a medal today when Porter reopens the University. You and I are looking for insight into your dad's last days, to solve a GRL riddle."

I picked up the packet.

"We don't have time to go through everything here," I said. "We need a quiet spot to figure out what's so important in here. And this ain't the spot. Annemarie is probably posting tweets about the Doc Watson story."

I put the package in my backpack. I had stowed my travel bag with a bellman back at the Carolina Inn. Maybe nobody would bother us back there at the hotel.

"Your defense. What time is the defense?" she asked.

"1:00 p.m. We have plenty of time," I said. "Do you have a room booked in your name at the Carolina Inn?"

"Yes, checked in late last night," she said.

"Okay. That's out. Everyone will have your name from the hotel registry," I said.

The longer we stood in the carrel, the more likely Pauley would be waiting to greet us.

"Let's walk," I said, and took Pearl's hand.

Chapter 44

Barbecue and gelato.
Our day in Chapel Hill.
We've had so many bad days.
A good one brings a thrill.

onday morning in October. Inside Racquetball Court No. 4. Fetzer Gym. 10:03 a.m.

A UNC student ID carries all kinds of access. We stopped to thank Annemarie on the way out.

"Did you find what you needed?" she asked.

"No, it was a dead end," Pearl said. She even made her voice crack for effect. "But thanks for trying."

Maybe that would slow down Twitter and Facebook.

We exited the library, walked past The Pit, which reminded me of the meeting Mallette requested for last Thursday. Makes sense now why he chose the location—right by his carrel, where he could pick up the package before our conversation. We moved down the steps and across the street; I used my ID to secure the racquetball court.

We sat down against a wall, and I pulled the package from my backpack, removed the contents, and spread everything out in front of us on the hardwood floor.

Inside the package, there were nine envelopes. One was a cream-colored letter-sized envelope addressed to Dr. Mallette. Return address for Dr. Beatriz Martins. Written in cursive. The envelope was sealed.

There were eight separate manila envelopes. Each one large enough to hold pages of standard printer paper without folding them. On the outside of each envelope, there was a nine-character code. A mix of numbers and capital letters from the English alphabet. Handwritten, again. Some kind of code or identification numbers. All of the envelopes were sealed with the gummy adhesive users have to dampen in order to make it stick.

Inside each envelope were two documents. Both printed from a computer. Both stapled in the upper left corner. Both in English. In each envelope, one of the documents had "translated" in the upper right corner. Handwritten. In each envelope, a second document had "published" in the upper right corner. Handwritten. Other than those notations in the upper right corner, at first glance, the documents looked the same.

"Dad never saw any of this," Pearl said.

It was like a reverse time capsule.

"Open the letter," she said, picking it up and putting it my hands.

I tore off a thin strip of paper on the short end of the envelope, where a stamp would have been placed—if the letter had been mailed instead of handed to Mallette directly.

Inside was a letter, printed from a computer, from Bea to Mallette. It was dated the previous Monday, the day prior to her last meeting with Mallette.

Dear Dr. Mallette:

I can't thank you enough for your assistance over the past few months. The tenure dispute has been painful, both personally and professionally. It's an embarrassing kind of thing, and I am grateful for the way you have helped me navigate the process with dignity.

Please know that I love the University and have a great relationship with my students. I am excited by the idea of extricating myself from roles that emphasize research so that I may contribute in areas better aligned with my strengths. I am passionate about young people and the opportunities that open up to them through new languages.

On a separate matter, I am sharing the enclosed journal articles with you so that you may pass on the material to Dr. Holly Pike. I understand you will see her this week as part of the University Day events.

The author of the articles, Dr. Rin Itou, hired me frequently to translate conference papers that she ultimately submitted to prestigious scientific journals. I kept copies of the published articles for my files. For my translation consulting business, the published articles are like the paintings in an artist's portfolio.

Recently, I noticed a few differences between one of the translated items and the published article. I went back to other works and found more discrepancies. I attempted to contact Dr. Itou earlier this year to confirm that the changes and alterations were not related to any failure on my end in the translation work. Translating statistical findings is the most challenging work I do. I never did hear back from her and then later learned she had been killed in an auto accident.

My husband, a statistician, reviewed the documents and indicates to me there was no issue with my translation work. But I would like confirmation with the appropriate GRL staff member so that I may be considered for future work.

I appreciate you sharing the material with Dr. Pike. I would be happy to speak with the new director of the Tokyo lab. It has been a great experience.

With great affection,

Bea

Chapter 45

We started out at Ye Olde.
Made our way to Back Bar late.
God bless the chicken biscuit.
And thank you for this date.

"Shit," Pearl said.

I folded the letter and slid it back in the envelope.

"What does it mean?" she asked. "Do you know what the stats say?"

"I don't know yet," I said. "I might. I might not. For a journalist, I'm a pretty good statistician. But for a statistician, I'm only an average journalist."

I picked up a pair of documents from one of the manila envelopes— an envelope marked 891LJD254. I did a quick scan of the version bearing the "translated" notation.

It was an article Rin produced related to the cellular engineering, presumably work that was leading up to SyNaptz. As best I could tell, the article reported on an experiment with rats. In one group, Rin treated rats with something like the insulin that diabetics use today. Based on periodic readings of the cellular data, the scientists added different levels of a synthetic insulin. They then tracked the sugar levels of the rats, some of which were fed healthy diets, and some fed a rat version of junk food.

With another set of rats, Rin tried something revolutionary: She started with cells she had modified in her lab. In these cells, she had inserted microchips. GRI's invention—in which Rin would share riches—was a chip scalable to a size so microscopic that it could essentially be written into the DNA of a cell. Rin took these cells and injected them into this second group of rats. Then, through her computer, Rin could order the cells to behave a certain way. That's what she did. She told the cells to behave as if they had been bathed in the synthetic insulin.

"I'm butchering the science," I said to Pearl. "But that's the best I can do. It's a space-age version of comparing Approach A to Approach B. To pick a winner."

Bea had made the comparison between the two papers easier. She had used a green highlighter to mark areas that differed in the "translated" and "published" documents.

Some of the differences were administrative. Some were only stylistic. Even I could see that. In the published version of diabetic rat paper, for example, the editors had cut down the literature review. All the same articles were cited in the bibliography. Rin just said it all in fewer words. Conference papers let writers be indulgent. I knew that from my own experience with conferences.

Some of the changes, on the other hand, looked like a big deal.

In the translated version, the bottom line was muddled. The rats with the fancy microchip cells did about as well as the rats receiving insulin. It was hard to make a comparison because the results were all over the map. The averages for both groups were about the same, but rats in the two groups had wildly different experiences.

"How could that work?" Pearl asked?

"Think about two classrooms of third-graders," I said. "Ten kids in each class. Teachers in both classes give pop quizzes this morning. In Classroom A, five kids get forty percent of the answers correct, and five kids get sixty percent of the answers correct. What's the average score for the class?"

"Okay. Class average is fifty," Pearl said.

"Now take Classroom B, five kids post a perfect score, one hundred percent. Five kids really bomb the test. Get absolutely nothing correct. They all score zero. What's the class average?"

"It's a tie," she said. "Both classes have the same score"

"That's sort of what happened with Rin's research. The translated article describes the crazy variation in the high-tech group and the stable performance of the insulin group. Best I can tell, it's still breathtaking research, even though the fancy rats don't do any better overall. It's what scientists do. They report on every incremental gain, every baby step along the way. And it's why social scientists get so revved up about variance and standard errors. Rin reports on that in the translated paper.

"Everything is different in the published paper. It focuses on the absolute difference in performance and relegates the variation to a footnote. And says the variations between methods require more investigation. That's true in the sense that everything requires more investigation."

"What would Rin say?" Pearl asked.

I had no idea. And I didn't want to try to speak for a dead GRL scientist who, even from the grave, would have a better handle on the science. I had no idea whether Mallette would have given the package to Fats, as asked. Or, if he did, would have reviewed the articles first, as we were doing. I had no idea what Fats would say.

"Assuming scientists are as prone to spin as politicians and jocks, I guess it's no shocker that the published version puffs up a bit," I said. "For any one article, I don't know that anyone would care. Might draw some attention from the *Times* as a gotcha piece. But nobody else.

"If it's a pattern, over years, across a series of high-stakes publications..." I said.

Pearl could see where I was headed.

"Sounds like something Wall Street would care about," she said. "You need to tell Dr. Pike."

"She hired me because she believes there is fraud," I said. "And she's paying me $5 million. I can't go back to her and tell her my big finding is that I believe there's fraud. I've got to pin down the fraud. If SyNaptz is based on an overreach from Rin, I need to have documentation for Fats. I don't want the *Today Show* springing something like this on her. It's my job to make certain she knows where any weak spots exist. So GRL can address the issues."

"Five million. Huh," Pearl said.

Chapter 46

Took up Bikram yoga,
and organic cigarettes.
Trying to minimize,
my maximum regret.

*I*t was past noon. We had been grinding through all of the articles. I really needed some hot tea. The more I read, the less I knew about the science. I could grasp the point of the articles only at the most superficial, conceptual level. There would usually be a line or two in the methods section and a line or two in the discussion of the results. Once I could grab on to some basic explanation, I could sort of "reverse-engineer" my way back through the rest of the piece.

What was easy to spot was that the pattern was more than spin for the scientific journals. The discrepancies were systematic, directional, and sweeping in scale. I imagine a content expert would call it fraud. It would at least merit attention from a blue-ribbon panel. Yet, if the threshold question was clear to me from this initial review, it was impossible to tell who was behind it. Rin? Partners at Tickle geeked up about SyNaptz? GRL editors trying to make headlines on CNN? No one could perform an autopsy on a journal article.

"I'm going to need more time with the data," I said, "but right now we need to get over to Gerrard. I know Porter wants you there, too."

Pearl put all the articles back in the original envelopes, then put everything, including the letter, back in the original package. She used the brass clip to secure the flap on the package. The adhesive was only good for one shot.

I stood on the hardwood floor of the court and stretched my back, my legs. I was going to be sitting in this defense for another long stretch.

I needed to get back into the GRL system. Poke around more. I wanted to type in the nine-character IDs on each article to see what comes up. I wanted to plug in Max's name and Bea's.

And Fats was ready to send me off to Budapest to find the fraud. I could save her a lot of time and money—and save her potential public humiliation—if I could locate the source of the mendacious science.

My GRL cell buzzed. A text from Fats.

"Looking forward to seeing you in Gerrard Hall, Dr. Battle. Will be good to see you in a starring role on stage."

"I'm on my way," I texted back.

"Let's meet up later at The Franklin," she texted back. "Started renovations at the place on Gimghoul. I have a suite at The Franklin—and an open tab at The Crunkleton! So let's celebrate your PhD and my hundred-million dollar donation."

"Deal," I wrote.

I put the package in my backpack. Checked my personal phone. Two texts from Siler.

First: "Jefferson sent over a rough cut of 'Blame the Pie.' Here's a link."

Second text: "I'm steering clear of the circus. Swing by here after the defense. Carla and I want to buy you a drink."

"My first post-doc drink is with you. See you soon," I wrote back.

Pearl and I headed across campus. Gerrard Hall was up ahead. There was a crowd outside. A line of satellite TV trucks on Cameron Avenue. We turned behind a building to be out of the sight lines of the trucks.

"Thanks for doing this," she said. "I know you don't have any interest in being part of the show. In the end, organizing your doctoral defense event in this manner is an authentic way to honor Dad. He loved the University rituals, and I know he's proud . . ."

I stopped walking. She didn't finish her sentence. She turned her back to me and wiped her eyes. She turned back around, her eyes shiny. She stepped close. Put her hand on my cheek. I felt a pop run from my neck down my spine. She leaned her forehead in, touching mine.

We came back around the corner. Set our eyes on Gerrard doorway and ignored the media. Through the door at 12:58 p.m.

Chapter 47

When I ask you how you're doing, I really don't want to know.
When I ask if you can come along, I really don't want you to go.

$\mathcal{M}$ onday afternoon in October. Pig Farm Tavern in Chapel Hill. 3:02 p.m.

I passed.

The event was uneventful.

Porter announced the reopening of the University. We could hear the bell tower chime through the open doors of the small building.

He announced the schedule for the public memorial service. Porter introduced the president, who announced Dr. Holly Pike as the new White House Science Advisor. She also announced a new White House initiative to promote public service among undergraduate students at campuses across the country. Dr. Holly Pike would be honorary chair of the initiative. Which led to the announcement of the $100 million gift to the University. Then, a photo op with Fats, Porter, and the president.

The press corps followed the White House crew, which is what we all hoped would happen, leaving the quad as close to normal as it had been in weeks. Students were back in large numbers moving from dorm to class—or to somewhere. At least, the campus was animated again.

The dissertation defense was simple and boring. All four committee members signed the page. Miller and Quail from Journalism & Mass Communication. Carter and Reed from Sociology. The fifth line was left blank. That is, until Pearl took the page and signed her own name. So much for protocol. Let the dean of the graduate school object.

We wrapped before the 2:30 target.

Pearl and I walked across the bricks, a meandering route so as to avoid any proximity to the crime scene. Passed by the Old Well. I took her hand and guided us toward the rose garden and sundial. Crossed Franklin Street and came up the back stairs into Pig Farm.

FBI had moved its command center out of the bar, so it was back to being a bar again. Whiskey bottles replaced coffee pots.

Siler and Carla were smiling. The pool table was covered with heavy plastic and then topped with a sheet of plywood, on which rested a sampling from the best local chefs. Pearl and I started with Bill Smith's Atlantic Beach Pie. John Prine was coming through the speakers.

Pearl kissed my check.

Pearl filled a plate to share. Sat in the back booth. Our spot. Siler came over and opened a bottle of 1926 Macallan whiskey.

"My goodness," Pearl said.

"Only forty bottles ever produced," Siler said. "Been poking around the auction houses, and this one came up recently. Got lucky with a bid."

"Saloon business must pay well," Pearl said, smelling the aroma of the dark single malt.

"Let's just assume Lassie will see this one on his Amex," Siler said.

"The price of telling your friend you have a $5 million consulting gig," I said. "Pour away."

It felt good to drink and laugh with old friends, knowing there was no paper, no test. No academic hoop through which I had to jump. I had cleared the last hurdle. As painful as it was for Mallette to miss it, it was special to have Pearl there.

She would turn to the left and squint her eyes when the whiskey burned down her throat. The V-neck in her sweater opened to her collarbone, which somehow was sexy. And she had the neck of a princess, made for a string of the gems for which she was named. The ruby stones in her earrings looked like they might start dripping red drops onto her shoulders. She kicked me under the table a couple of times. I began to hope it was on purpose.

With the FBI gone, Siler and Carla eventually had to tend to other customers.

Pearl stepped to the ladies room.

I opened my laptop. Three questions from the racquetball analysis were bugging me.

My GRL phone buzzed. A text from Fats.

"ETA?" She was waiting at The Crunkleton.

"Give me forty-five mins," I wrote back.

Chapter 48

Eve winked at Adam,
and right away she had him.
She never had to buy another drink.
With Eden full of whiskey,
it made the old boy frisky.
And on the eighth day he began to think.

I navigated back into the GRL system easily.

Pearl slid back into the booth. Across from me. Kicked me as she settled in.

"All work and no play," she said.

She swigged a Dos Equis. She had switched to beer after the dram of rare single malt.

"Somebody's gotta pay for the whiskey Siler is buying," I said.

"How about we work and play?" she asked. "Together."

She had brushed her hair back into the Grace Kelly look.

I explained I was doing a quick dive for three things.

First, is Dr. Beatriz Martins anywhere in the GRL system? I queried the GRL system to look in several spots. She was not in the HR system. So she had never been a full- or part-time employee, and she had not won a large contract with the corporation. GRL used a different system to track smaller vendors and individual consultants who may do work for individual labs. So the janitors cleaning the Lima office were not booked in the same HR database as big international research firms carrying out drug trials.

Bea showed up here. In the past three years, her annual fees ranged from $7,500 to $22,500. Not life-changing money, but critical cash for a woman whose spouse was running up gambling debts. All of the fees came through the Tokyo office, and Rin had signed off on all the payments. When she clicked on the approvals in the company's portal, it put an electronic time stamp on the transaction, including her initials "RI."

Siler was right all along. I needed to look at the network connections in the databases. Looking for individual actions didn't tell me as much about the fraud as the relationships between the actors. Understanding haystacks meant understanding how the needles connect to one another.

Second question: Is Max Whitehall in the GRL system anywhere? Not in the HR databases. Not in the tracking of vendors or consultants. Looked under some other rocks, and found nothing. Then a hit. In a kind of dead-letter file, I found a reference to "M. Whitehall." That name was logged as having submitted a letter to the editor for one the GRL journals—the journal publishing Rin's most high-profile work. With research journals, letters to the editor were not like the random complaint letters showing up in a daily newspaper. Journals usually use the letters to managing ongong methodological debates between authors and respondents, from one journal issue to the next. Max Whitehall had never published anything in any kind of GRL journal, so it made sense that his submission would not show up in an issue.

Once I found this dead-letter file, I saw lots of oddball submissions that would never show up in print. A professor from London wrote a letter to complain about the paper stock. A guy wrote in to complain that his fiancé dreamed of publishing in GRL journals more than going on their honeymoon. GRL could publish these online for laughs. For the "M. Whitehall" letter, I could see the editor's decision to direct the letter into the virtual junk file. I could see the folder created for the letter. Unlike the other funny letters, though, the "M. Whitehall" folder was empty.

I toggled out of the GRL system and over to Google. Searched for Whitehall's name. Embarrassed I hadn't done this earlier.

It would have been easier before the million articles hit about the government source identifying him as Mallette's killer. So I modified the search to look for hits occurring before the past week. Not much there. Not a very public guy. A couple of professional association connections. Like every adjunct professor, he had minor papers accepted by minor conferences. His were technical papers, focused on sleep-inducing statistics. But the titles of the papers made my heart jump. He had written about the "bootstrap" method of calculating standard errors. In his microscopic niche, Whitehall studied standard errors.

Then I saw his home address come up in the online White Pages. 417 Buttons Road.

"Damn, there's 4:17 again," I said out loud, but to myself.

"You're good at this," Pearl said.

"Imagine if I worked sober," I said. On my third dram of the whiskey that's worth its weight in gold.

"What's your third question?" she asked.

Curious if these nine-character codes are in the GRL system. I zipped open my backpack found a code on the top corner of one of the eight manila envelopes: 891LJD254.

Nothing in the HR system for vendors and consultants. Tried several different options in the portal for the GRL journals. Finally found the connection.

Every submission to a GRL journal receives a nine-character code. This ID sticks with the article throughout the peer-review processes and editorial process. Every submission receives a disposition. Some are rejected outright.

Those that make it to the peer-review stage receive one of four dispositions: publish as is; publish with modest revisions; re-consider for publication if the author will make substantial changes; or reject.

The first three of those dispositions lead to more branches on the decision tree, and so on. Every decision along the way is recorded electronically with a time stamp that attaches initials. It turns out much of the journal editing occurred in the Budapest office–regardless of whether any researchers from that lab were connected to the work. It seems GRL had created a hub of editorial processing in Budapest.

For articles that make it all the way through to actual publication, there were additional decisions on the back end related to graphic design, proof-reading, legal review, and more. The author signs away rights. Most all of this was coordinated out of Budapest. The author must attest to the originality of his or her contributions. All of these requirements generate time stamps notated with the initials of the

GRL staffer overseeing the work.

Once I found the queue, I could view new and old submissions. It was like looking at the MIT admissions funnel. The tiniest fraction of all submissions made it to publication. In fact, the biggest screen was the first one. Fewer than twenty percent of submissions ever made it to peer review.

Once in the peer review process, a senior GRL staffer facilitated input from outside experts and from GRL experts. The reviews were blind. Authors didn't know who was reviewing their papers. The reviewers didn't know who wrote the papers they were reviewing. The feedback was a mix of doctoral expertise and eighth--grade pettiness. After the peer-review process, for articles accepted for publication, the author information was re-attached for all of the steps on the back end.

I typed in one code after another, all eight of the long, random IDs from the packet Bea left.

For every one of these articles, a GRL staffer with initials "HP" had signed off on the articles after the final peer-review approval. No notes. No detail. Couldn't tell if "HP" review was invited by the journal editor. Or initiated by "HP." Maybe "HP"–assuming this was Fats–was tracking publications from supernova researchers who have revenue deals from patents. No way to tell. All I could see was the time stamp. After peer-review and before the proofreading and graphic design stages.

My GRL phone buzzed. I didn't need to look at it.

"I'm late," I said. "Gotta go see Fats–uh, Dr. Pike."

Pearl looked at me but didn't move. With the funeral over and the

Porter ceremony wrapped, I realized Pearl didn't need me anymore. Didn't know if she was headed back to Maine. Or sticking here. Maybe she didn't know. She saw the question on my face.

"House on Friendly Lane is still a crime scene," she said. Then whispered: "My guess is they're turning the place upside down looking for the packet in your backpack."

"Ouch."

"No, no. Didn't mean that to sound like a complaint," she said. "I'm glad we have it. Just saying I'm going to be at the Carolina Inn for a few more days."

"Hey, do this for me," I said.

Then I restarted: "I know I can't ask you do to anything. But do you mind hanging here? Talk to Carla. We may want to borrow her car. I'll buzz you in a few."

"You got it—on one condition. I want to hear that song about the woman who is a Baptist and a Communist," Pearl said.

"Done," I said.

Which meant I'd have to write the damn song now.

"You need a ride to The Franklin?" Pearl asked.

"I doubt it," I said. Closed up the laptop and walked down the front stairs.

My hunch was right. A big Coulee was waiting for me. Driver waved me over. My footsteps on the sidewalk were louder than the car.

Chapter 49

I need over-draft protection
At the Karma Bank of Life.
I get more than I give.
And I specialize in vice.

The gods are gonna catch me.
And make me pay my debt.
I know the clock is running out.
But they ain't found me yet..

*F*ats looked unbelievably good. Her black pearls matched her hair. Her little red dress matched her lips. She was wearing hotel slippers but had black spike heels by the door of her suite. Her skin looked like the inside of an oyster shell.

She was pissed.

"I realize you're Dr. Battle now," she said, "but I don't pay people $5 million to make me wait."

When the driver curbed the Coulee by the hotel, I first walked across to The Crunkleton looking for Fats. So I was doubly late. My quick look into the saloon turned into a conversation with the bartender. He had been back in the storage area looking for a bottle of something Fats wanted. Some kind of gift. Promised her he would send it over if he found it.

"You're right," I said. "I apologize. It was unprofessional, and you deserve better."

I believe she had expected more of a fight. The muscles in her jaw relaxed–even more so when I held up the bottle The Crunkleton asked me to ferry over. Delamain cognac. It shimmered gold, like syrup.

"I have a fund-raiser later. Ackland Art Museum. I don't have much time," she said, taking the bottle and putting it to the side as she talked. "Give me a briefing on your GRL fraud work. And I need you in Budapest this week."

Fats took a seat in her desk chair and propped her feet on coffee table. The suite was nothing like Atlanta, but there was an office area that was separate from the bedroom, which was separate from the living room. We were in the office. All three rooms were aligned along Franklin Street. Each room had its own balcony. The door was open a couple of inches, and cool air blew in.

I did what all journalists do when their editors try to pin them down. I told half the story.

"Picking up on what you know from our Atlanta briefing," I began, "I can confirm that a disproportionate share of editorial decisions are coming from the Budapest lab. That, plus the SEC charges and the eight hits on my analysis confirm that we need to look closely there."

I paused.

"Keep going," she said.

"I'm studying all the processes associated with the author submissions, peer review, and editorial decisions. I will create a visual map of the points at which fraud is possible. Then attach probabilities–based on my take–for fraudulent activity occurring at each point. Then I'll compare my estimates against input from your team. The trick is to translate a fuzzy, amorphous notion–*fraud*–into something discrete and quantifiable. It's essentially a set of decision trees, and we need to see what controls are in place to reduce the chances of fraud at each step."

"Give me an example," she said.

As I formulated an example, Fats woke up her iPhone and dialed. Whoever answered was used to taking orders. She offered no greeting.

"Swing around to the ABC store. Or Siler's. Bring us a bottle of Bulleit Rye"

She hung up. Fats wagged her finger at me when she saw me look at the Delamain bottle, wondering why she had ordered the rye when we were swimming in cognac.

"Focus on me, not the bottle," she said. "Again: an example?"

"So fraud cannot emerge on its own at random stages during the publishing process. It's not like fruit rotting in a bowl, where it's good one day and bad the next. It's like someone sticking a razor blade in a piece of fruit. It's not there. Then later it is. It requires a human being to create the fraud."

"Keep going," she said.

"So an author submitting an article can cook up fake findings before he or she ever sends the piece to GRL for consideration. That would be one point. The peer-review process is another spot when fraud could occur. The blind-review method is a control to guard against that. The graphic design process is another time. And so on. And fraud could occur in either direction. An author could submit a bad paper to GRL, which challenges your review process to uncover the corruption. Or an author could submit a straight paper to GRL journals, and then fraud could be introduced during the review and editing process."

That was as far as I was willing to go.

"More?" she asked.

"That's all I've got right now," I said.

"We need this map and the decision tree. You've found a point of weakness in our system. It's bad we didn't have this in place already. Thank you," she said.

A knock on her door. Fats padded across the room and came back with tray of Bulleit Rye, ice, and glasses.

I stood up and helped her with the tray.

She poured. She raised her glass.

"To Dr. Battle," she said.

The rye was pungent on my tongue after the rare Macallan. But very good.

She took a big sip.

Then another.

Then she put her glass down. Reached behind her neck. I heard a zipper move. Then the red dress fell to the hotel floor like an anchor through still water.

There was not a textile left on her body.

She stood on the coffee table and kissed me on the mouth, towering over me as if her wealth and power gave her height.

"You have the arts thing," I said, catching air in between kisses. "You told them you would be there."

"What's one more lie?" she said, leaping from the coffee table with her legs wrapped around my waist. We bounced off the chair and onto the floor, like freshmen in a dorm room with no bed.

Chapter 50

My calendar's torn, and my mind has grown worn.
I've lost all track of the time.
I slept on the floor. I shouldn't do that no more.
And I gotta stop doing those lines.

It was fun without the blindfold, too.

Fats was remarkably fit. Her triathlon training showed in the tone of her muscles and in her aerobic stamina.

When I was spent, I was certain she was not. But she was kind. She pulled cushions off the chair and propped under our heads. We were tangled, wet, and sweaty. Completing some weird lifecycle event, having made love like this as twenty-year-old romantics and now as fifty-year-old friends. In so many ways, it was better. What was lost in the folds of skin and the huffing and puffing–speaking of myself, now–seemed small compared to what we gained through attentiveness and fearlessness.

She tried to drink more whiskey lying down and poured a good bit down her neck. I licked off her neck and breasts.

She laughed.

It was past 9 p.m. now.

"This art thing isn't happening," she said. "Hand me my phone."

She pressed her thumb to the screen. The iPhone woke up. She opened the text editor and sent a note to the event coordinator.

"Congratulations on a great event. My gift is in the mail. Sorry I can't get to the party," she texted.

She put the phone down. Then wrote out a $50,000 check to Ackland. Fats paired it with the Delamain and rang her service. Directed the guy to deliver the bottle and the check to the museum director.

"Now, then," she said. She switched from work to play.

Set upright and pulled the rye over to our side of the coffee table. Poured herself a new glass and took half of it in.

She put my hand between her legs and together we orchestrated another climax for her. Then she fell asleep in the crook of my elbow, the chair cushion beneath her billion-dollar brunette hair.

I dozed off briefly and dreamed of data streaming through my brain, as if a John Nash vision had overtaken me. I saw curvilinear data mapping flights of cardinals looking for food in winter. Blossoming heat maps describing the carbon footprint of big cities. Sweeping animations showing the diminishing California aquifers. Spiraling algorithms measuring John Lennon's art and Ava Gardner's beauty.

Then a data point flashed into my brain that shot me awake. It scraped over my brain like a kitchen match on a roofing shingle. Every distraction dissolved. The back of my neck was suddenly filled with cold sweat against the cushion.

It was past midnight.

There was a data point I needed. I tried to wish it away, but couldn't.

Fats was sound asleep. My left arm under her neck. I reached my right arm over her waist, to where she had set aside her phone.

This was the gamble of all gambles.

I tapped the phone to get to the log-on screen. Carefully manipulated the screen around in my hand. With all the love I could find, I softly pressed the glass screen to her thumb.

The phone woke up.

A Coulee is a car made for a scientist, Fats had told me. The car self-reports on its operations. Sends her weekly texts. A black box, like an electronic data recorder, just like Delta has on airplanes.

I opened the text editor.

A sorrowful text from the arts fundraiser guy pretending to miss her at the event. When all he wanted was the gift.

Several text threads of no business import. One thread with me. Another with Darby. TV Heartthrob Guy again, asking about some doc film opening in New York.

Lots of work texts related to schedules. Seems a CEO devotes most of her time to managing her time.

Then the text thread from Coulee. Three recent texts. Each coming on a Sunday night. Each text one week apart.

Working the phone with my right hand, opened the most recent text.

From last night.

Lots of happy talk about the joys of being a Coulee owner. Some kind of dashboard with basic metrics about the car's performance over the past week. Measures of electricity used. Miles driven, and so on. Looked more like data from a laptop than a car. No traditional MPG data, of course.

Scrolled down. Prayed my hunch would not pay off. Felt more cold sweat on my neck.

There it was: A link to "daily activity."

Chapter 51

Jack be nimble, and be quick.
Someone took my cinnamon sticks.

Black cat crossed me twice this week.
A hat on the bed and a crow in the street.

clicked through several layers then got to the daily log. Started with Monday–one week ago today.

There it was. Last Monday evening. The big Coulee was parked outside of Pig Farm. Then motored late back to Gimghoul Road.

Skipped past Tuesday. Past Wednesday.

Fats nuzzled deeper into my neck. Her soft breasts pressed against my skin.

The link for Thursday was on the screen.

Coulee reported haystacks of data. I hoped there was no needle here.

I punched the link. The log had stored early morning activity.

At 4:22 a.m., the Coulee moved silently from Gimghoul Road to a parking space on the street by the old post office.

Then the machine rolled west just a bit, and at the far edge of Battle Hall pulled into the narrow drive of University Methodist Church. It parked in the small lot tucked away behind the church, behind Hyde Hall. As close as a car could get to the Caldwell memorial without ruining the grass.

At 4:54 a.m., the rolling computer moved in silence down East Franklin Street, through campus, to Country Club Road. Then onto Laurel Hill. Stopping on Buttons Road. 417 Buttons Road.

I nearly screamed.

I emailed the links to myself.

Then I very slowly pulled my left arm free. Used two hands to take a screen shot from the phone. Then emailed the JPG to myself.

I backed the phone out of the links and out of the text editor, back to the home screen. Then locked it again. Reached my arm over Fats and put the phone back where she had left it.

Kissed her on the cheek as I began to move.

She ran her hand up and down my leg. She nodded half awake as I got to my feet.

"Hey, there," I said.

I reached my arms up to the ceiling, up on my toes. As if to stretch myself awake from a deep sleep. Pulled a fleece cover off the back of the sofa and covered Fats. Reached and grabbed my clothes and backpack.

"I'm going to get biscuits," I said. "Back in just a few."

I moved out of the room in silence, my heart frozen.

Chapter 52

Triskaidekaphobia, this is my lucky day.
Found an angel here on earth, in the strangest way.

finished dressing in the elevator. Made it to the hotel lobby. Stayed away from the front windows. I could see the Coulee and black car out front.

I opened my personal phone and called Pearl's number.

She answered before the first ring quit.

"You okay?" she said right off.

"Not really. Well, yes. Or I will be," I stammered. "We're going to make it okay. Did you arrange for Carla's car? Not one of Siler's old BMWs, but Carla's Subaru?"

"Yes, I have her keys here."

"Perfect. Need you to pick me up. But don't come down Franklin Street. Come down Cameron Avenue. Pick me up at the corner of Cameron and Mallette," I said.

"This some kind of joke?" she asked.

It didn't hit me that I was directing her to a street named for her late father's grandfather.

"For real. I'll explain when I see you. Just stay off West Franklin," I said. "I'm leaving the hotel through the garage and walking up Mallette Street. I'll be at the corner. You come down Cameron."

"Why the drama?" she said.

"You wouldn't believe me if I told you. Just come," I said. Clicked off.

I moved through the garage and got to Mallette Street without disturbing the Coulee or the black car. The walk up to Cameron was cold. Groups of sorority sisters were coming down the sidewalk.

I realized I was carrying a black box that would track my movements–the GRL issued iPhone.

"Excuse me," I said to a thicket of coeds. "Kind of a crazy thing here. Here's a new iPhone that I found on the sidewalk here. Wondering if one of you may have lost one? Or if you could add it to the lost-and-found box at your house?"

Most of the young women were quiet.

One leader stepped up.

"Sure," she said. Reached out and took it from my hand.

Either she was doing a good deed or wanted a free phone. I didn't care which. Let the GRL spies watch the phone bounce from party to party.

Pearl was at the corner five minutes after I got there.

"Go," I said. "Toward Greensboro."

She kept it in park. Stared at me.

"I promise I will explain. I can also promise you this is life and death. Just go," I said.

As Pearl moved through Carrboro and toward the Interstate, I called Siler on my cell. Spoke to him and to Carla. Confirmed that the Valle Crucis house was still in shape for guests. Told Carla to count on us being there for at least a week. Probably two. Maybe more.

Asked her not to perjure herself with the feds but otherwise not tell anyone where we were located.

Then called my old editor at the *Post*.

"Houston, it's me," I said into his voice mail. "Get the fuck out of bed and call me back." Left him my cell number. Then texted it to him.

Had an email from my parents. They caught a live internet connection in Kiev and just read about Mallette's murder, the FBI tying up the case with Whitehall as killer, and then the University reopening today with my defense.

"Congratulations, Dr. Battle," Dad emailed. "You honored Dr. Mallette in a special way."

"It has been a week like no other," I wrote back, which was the most economical way to explain what was going on. "I'm headed to Valle Crucis for a few days. Expect to see my take on events in the *Post* within a week or two. The story is as spectacular as it is sad."

"Not another mile," Pearl said.

She had pulled off into the parking lot of burger joint by the interstate.

"I will go to Valle Crucis with you. I will go to the end of the earth with you. I will drink whiskey with you from now until the end of time," she said. "But only if you tell me what is going on."

Chapter 53

All my underwear's dirty, and my fuel light's blinking.
I've got three dollar bills, I spent the rest drinking.
I've gone through my boxers, and my fuel light's blinking.
I've got three crinkled bills, and I gotta stop drinking.

*T*uesday night in October. Mast General Store, Valle Crucis. 8:02 p.m.

Pearl was on the porch, enjoying an unseasonably mild October evening. She was ahead of me on several measures, namely shopping trips and drinks.

We got to Siler's house somewhere close to 5:00 a.m. I was on the phone with Houston for the last hour of the trip, negotiating the deal.

I told Houston I would go on the record as source in solving the Mallette murder and in bringing down a Fortune 100 CEO—and revealing the truth about SyNaptz, a bio-tech innovation that would otherwise sail through testing into public use.

Houston, of course, pointed out that the Mallette murder had been solved. The whole world knows Max Whitehall's name. He was a murderer.

Which forced me to say in front of Pearl what I had recognized days ago but not wanted to point out to her until I had no other choice: That Pauley and the FBI were having it both ways. They were leaking accusations about Whitehall, allowing reporters to give credit to "sources close to the federal investigation." At the same time, they didn't present a public case against Whitehall, and they kept Mallette's office, house, and University residence secured as crime scenes. And now Buttons Road. The campus assumed the case was closed because the public security presence was gone, and the University reopened. But only the security cops posted by all the dorms and classroom buildings were sent home. The crime scene investigators were still working around the clock.

I knew the Whitehall headlines were giving Pearl some closure, and I didn't want to unravel it for her. Until I could present an alternative theory. I told Houston I could deliver that to him.

Pearl could piece together enough of this from hearing my side of the conversation. Tears rolled down her face while she drove us into the mountains, into safety.

"Okay," Houston said. "You got my attention."

"In exchange for going on the record as a source and laying out the case for you," I said, "I want space for a first-person piece."

Houston was silent.

"It will run under a double byline—my name and Sanders Mallette," I said. "I'm working from notes he made, and I'm writing the final piece. Both our names will be on it."

"On the condition that whatever you write has to clear our editorial standards, like everything else we publish, you've got a deal," he said.

"I'll set forth the case in writing and email you later this morning," I said. "Then whoever you have writing lead can call my cell to interview me. I'll have the first person to you in the afternoon."

We both clicked off.

Pearl had taken the car out for a shopping trip while I was writing through the morning. She napped, showered, and put on her new jeans and fleece while I was talking to the Post, then writing the first-person piece.

She dropped off a new shirt and jacket for me before heading to Mast. I did the half-hour walk to get there. First time I had moved my legs much in twenty-four hours. The physical clarity felt good. I was already at peace in my mind.

"The *Post* has everything now?" she asked.

I sat down in the rocking chair beside her. She handed me a beer.

"Yep."

"And you think we're better off going this route, instead of going to Pauley?" she asked.

This was a tough one. I believed I was lucky to have the journalism route available.

"Most people are stuck with one option in this kind of situation," I said. "Which is the same as no option. They'd have to go to Pauley. He knows that, and it gives him all the leverage. Pauley would take everything we shared and probably bury it. Or do whatever would make the

FBI look good. Easy to hang it on Whitehall. Tough to take on GRL."

"Nowadays, technology has created a second option for some people. Snowden showed that there's some power in dumping all the data into the public domain. Let the world sort it all out. I just don't have that much faith in the sorting power of the public."

"You think you've got a third way?" she asked.

"I do. I'm lucky. The *Post* has enough credibility to force Pauley to confront the facts publicly," I said. "And the Post has a megaphone big enough to put things in public view. Sunlight will prevent Pauley from burying inconvenient truths."

"But the *Post* can't just print your version of the case," she said.

"Correct," I said. "That's why I told Houston I'd go on the record as a source. I used to be a newspaper reporter. In this deal, I'm the newsmaker. Not the reporter.

"Reporters need credible sources. I'm offering myself up for this role. Based on the case I set forth, the documentary evidence I provide and my on-the-record interview, the *Post* will go to Pauley with questions. And the *Post* can use the documents I send to seek out independent verification. All of this will force Pauley to make a choice. I'm backing he'll play it like he knew all of this already. He'll act pissed off the *Post* has it, but he'll take credit for the solve. He's not wired to admit he needed a washed-up reporter to figure it out for him."

"And the first-person piece?" she asked.

"I wrote a commentary piece," I said. "I'm on the byline with your dad. It'll run separate from the news piece."

We moved inside. Sat in varnished old rocking chairs chairs near a hot stove.

"I don't want to read it in the *Post*," Pearl said. "Tell me what happened. Tell me your theory of the case."

Chapter 54

I dream we dance away the day.
At Big Rock Candy Mountain.
The Hot Band plays from all the steeples.
And my heart's on fire again.

From the hour of darkness.
I hear her voice on the whippoorwill.
She's never called me by my name.
And she never will.

*P*eople kill for money, love, or power.

Dr. Holly Pike was two for three. She killed for money and power.

The drive she used to make her first billion, and her second and third, and to move up the Forbes list, is the same drive that pushed her to chase the impossible: to turn human cells into little computers. The obsession turned a worthy aspiration into a foregone conclusion. Fats already decided that the bio-tech product would become real. When the facts didn't support her foregone conclusions–which formed the predicate she sold to investors–she had to contrive a paper trail of research suited to the future she desired.

This all started when Fats picked off Rin's early research on biologics and cellular engineering. Fats saw promise in the work that Rin could not have imagined.

Whereas Rin initially was satisfied with the authentic, incremental gains of scientific findings, Fats saw a vision for SyNaptz. So she puffed up the findings and downplayed the cautions, spinning the stats to her advantage and in some cases playing with the analyses in ways that rose to fraud. Rin went along because Fats made her rich, made her an international star. Getting a tech giant like Tickle on board sealed the deal.

Once Fats had established a research trail sufficient to attract capital for a new round of funding, she orchestrated Rin's murder. At that point, Rin offered no new value and created potential exposure. An auto accident in Tokyo was easy.

The Bootstrap emails were a loose end. They started when Max Whitehall figured out something screwy was occurring with Rin's research. He didn't know anything about the science, but he knew enough statistics to see the pattern.

Fats missed some details here. She missed that translation services are not handled through centralized GRL consulting contracts. These are handled lab by lab, outside of the tightly controlled publication and peer-review contractor processes. Bea took a lot of pride in this translation work, and she saved the journal articles for her portfolio–as a clip file to promote her skill to prospective clients. When she saw the discrepancies between what she translated and what was published, her first concern was that she was screwing up some of the technical work. She didn't want to lose work because of problems translating the stats.

She checked first with her husband, a stats instructor. He correctly assured her that her translation skill was not at issue here.

What he didn't tell her is that he tried to blackmail GRL with the information.

It was the crazy, stupid move of a degenerate gambler making his last bet on a longshot. Even if GRL didn't kill him, it could have smothered him. Made him irrelevant. He was delusional. He was clumsy.

Most of all, he was ineffective. He got Mallette killed and got his wife killed. And got himself killed.

When Fats figured out the emails were coming from Max–and the letter to the editor submitted through the online portal didn't help–he was a dead man. Fats re-connected with Mallette to open discussions about a new gift to the University. She bought the house in Chapel Hill. All to give her proximity to Max.

Then she saw how frequently Bea was meeting with Mallette. And Rose mentioned to her that Bea left a package for Mallette when she met with him on Tuesday.

Fats decided to take everyone out. She told Mallette she'd meet him for a pre-dawn walk through campus. He was waiting for her at Caldwell. She killed him. She had access to plenty of knitting needles through her lover in Atlanta, an artist working with textiles. She then moved her silent car to Buttons Road, where she shot Bea and then put the gun in Max's mouth, under threat. She put his hand on the handle and pulled the trigger.

With Tickle, Fats planned to spin off the SyNaptz biologics business in January, with an IPO sure to follow. This would bring billions–not millions, but billions–to Fats and her investors.

Even better, it would put her in line for a Nobel Prize and make her the most famous scientist in the world.

"How will Pauley react when the *Post* offers up this theory?" Pearl asked.

"He'd blow it out of the water if there were nothing but speculation," I said. "But I've sent the *Post* my files, all my data. Scanned in all of the pages from the package and sent those. Sent the times and addresses of the Coulee report. Not sure the link to Coulee data will work for the *Post*, but the paper can report that that its source viewed the data directly. The FBI can ignore it or subpoena the black box. Pauley can claim I created the JPG. But he won't be comfortable with the bluff."

We opened fresh beers.

"I gave the *Post* everything but the gun. I expect she tossed that in a dumpster somewhere in Atlanta, but who knows," I said.

"So why would Holly hire you?" she asked.

"Easy," I said. "She wanted to know how much exposure, if any, GRL had on the new bio-tech business. The media attention, and eventually the IPO, would draw every kind of skeptic in the world. If I couldn't find the fraud, she figured she'd be in the clear. If I did find the fraud, she could pin it on Rin and manage the damage before the SyNaptz IPO. She could get out ahead of the story and explain away the problem as a rogue researcher. Even with Bea's package, I never would have had anything real on Fats without the Coulee data."

"Glad she didn't buy a Porsche," Pearl said.

Epilogue

She's the feminist I want to kiss.
A Baptist and a Communist.

She's got immunity from powers that be.
Winks at the sheriff, he pretends he doesn't see.

Keeps her bullets with her Bible.
Doesn't shave above her knee.

Wears a scarf she stole from Newport,
and a ring from Galilee.

She's a Baptist and a Communist.
Shot her man when he raised his fist.

She's the feminist I want to kiss.
A Baptist and a Communist.
A Baptist and a Communist.

She's got a happy face but under those bangs,
her mind is always working to facilitate some change.

Organizing hotel maids,
marching for a living wage.

By the jail she kneels and whispers,
Oh, God please calm my rage

She's a Baptist and a Communist.
Shot her man when he raised his fist.
She's the feminist I want to kiss.
A Baptist and a Communist.
A Baptist and a Communist.

*M*onday night in April. Pig Farm Tavern in Chapel Hill. 10:37 p.m.

With all due respect to my old friend Mallette, April is my favorite time of year in Chapel Hill.

My new bride, Pearl, is on stage introducing Jefferson Hart. He will open his show with "She's a Baptist and a Communist," my new song that's doing pretty well on the Americana charts.

This is a big night. Our one-month anniversary. The last loose ends from the events of last October are playing out. Last week, Trustees of Columbia University, in announcing the Pulitzer winners, picked our work in the *Post* for the commentary award. Turns out, I was able to craft a series of pieces examining cultural forces driving the grow-ing number of cases of Big Pharma using supposedly independent journals as a cover for fraudulent research that would generate huge profits–but never deliver benefits to sick patients. With Mallette's name on the byline, this was his third Pulitzer. My second.

The University offered me a faculty position, the Sanders Mallette Professor of Sociology and Journalism. I said I'd take the job if it came with tenure. Trustees agreed, so I now have a sinecure. The new gig starts in the fall. I'm designing a course called "Haystacks and Needles" that integrates narrative reporting into quantitative and qualitative data analysis.

Pearl and I will visit Kiev before I start the fall semester, to see my folks.

For the first time in my life, without any real reason, I've become a magnet for money. In addition to "She's a Baptist and a Communist," I fell into more good fortune when a recording star loved by teens worldwide turned "Snow Day" into a hit dance number. So raise a glass to Teen Idol. The cash register is ringing from that one.

The *Post* ran its news story a week after I downloaded the case to the paper, giving Pauley days to backfill and scramble his way to the front of the story. He spotted the way the wind was blowing and set his sails like a pro.

The GRL story dwarfed every previous corporate scandal. There was sex, murder, fraud, and a starlet CEO who was always camera ready. And a freaky, Orwellian plot line about Tickle and SyNaptz in charge of tiny computers running the cells in our bodies.

The company's board of directors responded with extraordinary sophistication, embracing the true facts and separating the company from Fats. The board made a strong case to investors that GRL was a profitable, well-run company–and the board compartmentalized the SyNaptz spinoff as a personal indulgence of the founder. The board published retractions to Rin's series of breakthrough articles and also published the original versions of her papers. The more limited findings would never have been enough to attract new capital but were more than sufficient to stimulate new research and new scholarship. Which was supposed to be the point. The board made a public commitment to pursue the cellular solutions through "honest scholarship, not contrived urgency."

Some PR firm got paid well for that one.

The board elected to pay me the balance of the $5 million contract.

I objected. Seemed crazy for the board to pay me to bring down its company.

The board, by unanimous vote, saw it the other way. Only by honoring the contract to search out the fraud could the board publicly demonstrate its commitment to honest research–and distance itself from Fats, at the same time.

Pearl and I waited in line at the credit union drive-through window, and I deposited a check for $3.75 million into my checking.

The timing was good. Pearl was the executrix of her dad's estate. So she really needed to sell the Friendly Lane house. She wasn't in a position to keep up the maintenance. The roofing needs alone would break her. And she had a responsibility to the estate to get value.

So I took a chunk of my cash and bought Mallette's Queen Anne house from the estate.

The estate then distributed its assets to Pearl, which put most of that cash into her pocket.

Then we moved in. So she went from being house-rich and cash-poor to being rich on both. And I picked up responsibility for maintenance.

Pearl, because she is an angel, then wrote a big check to the mission program my mom and dad are leading. She says the big donation will help offset some of the taxable income that keeps rolling in. We'll use our Kiev trip to see how Mom and Dad are spending the money. They finally caught up with the details when I mailed them a hard copy of the *Post's* coverage.

In January, Pauley was promoted to Deputy Director of the Bureau. I sent him a Teen Idol greatest hits CD.

Houston said Pauley was ready to shoot up the *Post* newsroom when the reporters called out of the blue seeking comment on my version of the Mallette case and the supporting evidence.

The *Post's* attorney called and said I would be charged with obstruction of justice, based on my decision to remove Bea's package from the carrel. The *Post's* attorney was rooting for this to happen, because he wanted to get Pauley on the witness stand and ask him why 200 agents neglected to check on whether the chancellor of the University–who'd been a faculty member for years–ever went to the library. When asked, Annemarie and others reported seeing him there daily. There was a carrel key on Mallette's keychain. The FBI was consumed with the office, Friendly Lane house, and Quail Hill. Mallette was hiding in plain sight.

Given that I turned over the evidence–however indirectly–within twenty-four hours, Pauley would have struggled to prove that my actions slowed down his. The bigger embarrassment, which Pauley managed to minimize by cooperating with the *Post*, was how FBI agents let GRL security drive the crime-scene investigations. The *Post's* public-records requests showed inventory lists on GRL letterhead, not FBI forms. Fats had ordered GRL agents to do whatever was necessary to find the package from Bea.

Fats was in custody, awaiting trial on first-degree murder charges. Three counts. The SEC came along with indictments, also, but it is the murder trial that has the potential for breakout TV ratings. National media types are speculating that she will take a plea deal; the chatter holds that the state of North Carolina may want to avoid the time and cost of a triple-murder trial that will take forever. I doubt Fats will plead to anything. I received communication from her, through her attorney, asking if I wanted to collaborate with her on a book project on the case. She believes in herself like no one in the world.

Pearl is keeping the Maine house as a summer vacation spot–or we're keeping it, I guess. What's mine is hers, and so forth. I dumped my rental in Westwood, and Pearl and I have everything we own in the Queen Anne or in the Maine house. She's also holding onto the two family plots in the old cemetery on campus. So we've lined up the last piece of real estate we'll ever own.

Pearl is chairing the board for the Mallette Center for Public Service. I was shocked that Fats didn't put a stop-payment on the $100 million check. The University initially announced it would return the gift, not wanting to take cash from the woman who murdered Mallette. Pearl made that an easy call, demanding that the University take the $100 million and sue Fats for more.

I guess I did help Fats, without really wanting to do so. When she was charged, she deeded the Gimghoul Road house to her attorney. The attorney immediately listed the property, turning the house into his fee. I bought it for Siler and Carla. I wanted the Coulee with the house, but the feds took the car as evidence.

Up on the stage tonight introducing Jefferson and his band, Pearl looks at peace. It reminds me of the image I get when I see her at the Southern Historical Collection, where she's helping to curate her dad's papers. The archivists have her wearing white cotton gloves and working in a secured room. She keeps her hair pulled back. I can see her through the privacy glass, and the ripples in the glass create an effect like an old film. I'm still distracted by the way sweaters hug her shoulders. Pearl has an electricity to her touch, one that I believe emanates from the flecks in her green eyes.

I still dream of lightning and the shipwreck ghosts protecting me on the shore, fire in the sky above the the sea. I am selfish with Pearl's gifts. When I grow weak, I take energy from her. When I lose my temper, I take grace from her. When I fail to repress ambition, I take empathy from her. Pearl sleeps on her side, and I lean my forehead in to hers. In those nights when sleep won't come to me, I touch the hard bone at the front of my skull to hers. I look at the tops of her eyelids and match the rise and fall of her breathing. I see the uncovered skin. No make-up, no dirt, no pretense, or latent worry. Every muscle in her neck as relaxed as an infant's. It's the bliss that comes to those who insist on reaching their hands into the future, grabbing onto tomorrow, and pulling themselves out of history, out of what has been, and fully into unmet possibilities. To those of us who live in the past, who carry on feuds with unseen ghosts from forgotten graveyards, Pearl is a savior.

We were married on Roanoke Island, on the North Carolina Outer Banks. I had suggested Deep Gap, her father's birthplace, because I devote that portion of my consciousness to the past. Pearl picked a spot she had never visited, again reaching into the future and dragging me along. I did contribute one element to our new future. Packing for Roanoke, I found a flat package wrapped in cotton and wool braids. Beautiful fabrics. I offered the gift to Pearl on our wedding night, after we had satisfied appetites for food and drink.

"It's a surprise package from a friend of a friend," I said. "I don't really know what is in the box myself. Though I have some guesses."

Pearl disassembled the wrapping without cutting the outer skin of cotton and wool. The braids were designed to come apart, like a puzzle. Inside were two, cashmere hand-made sleep masks. Which reminds me: We owe Darby a thank you note.

The Lassie James Songbook

Word & Music by John Bare & Don Dixon

1. Fair-Skinned Brunette

2. How Do You Like Your Eggs

3. She's a Baptist and a Communist

4. The Displaced Man

5. Whiskey Kisses

6. I Fell in Love with Emmylou

7. Do You Like to Slow Dance?

8. Brownsville Tonight

9. Redhead from Detroit

10. Is Today Monday?

11. No Songs About Mamas or Trains

12. Bougainvillea Blues

Fair-Skinned Brunette

By Don Dixon & John Bare © 2018

There is a fair-skinned brunette, she plants in the spring

She wears a big hat to keep her cheeks soft

Her shoulders get red in the Halifax sun

She appears in my dreams when angels carry me off

She hangs her jeans on her hips

And sheets on the line

That fair-skinned brunette

With the porcelain shine

There is a fair-skinned brunette who curses in French

She winked at me once from an old white Corvette

I showed her the stars and she cried at Orion

We poured Tullamore and sang some Tammy Wynette

She hangs her jeans on her hips

And sheets on the line

That fair-skinned brunette

With the porcelain shine

There is a fair-skinned brunette who finds malachite stones

Blends her own paints with kaolin clay

She flashes her temper - oh she flashes that temper - at squirrels in her garden

oohhhh

I rub down her scars when the light breaks each day

She hangs her jeans on her hips

And sheets on the line

That fair-skinned brunette

With the porcelain shine

Fair-skinned brunette

With the porcelain shine

How Do You Like Your Eggs?

By Don Dixon & John Bare © 2018

I don't care if you believe in God

I don't care if you like cats or dogs

I don't care how you raise your boys

And I don't care about my toys

I don't care if you shave your legs

All I wanna know ... is how do you like your eggs

Benedict or quiche

Pickled, poached or fried

On a biscuit with some cheese

Scrambled, baked or ... Shirred

How do you like your eggs

How do you like your eggs

How do you like your eggs

On Sunday morning.

I'll shop for window treatments

I take you to the mall

You can pick out kitchen counter tops

Cause I don't care at all

I don't care at all

I don't care if you shave your legs

All I wanna know ... is how do you like your eggs

Benedict or quiche

Pickled, poached or fried

On a biscuit with some cheese

Scrambled, baked or ... Shirred

How do you like your eggs

How do you like your eggs

How do you like your eggs

On Sunday morning.

How do you like your eggs

How do you like your eggs

How do you like your eggs

On Sunday morning.

Sunday Morning.

Ohhh, ooh, doodle, do to do to

Ohhh, ooh

She's a Baptist and a Communist

By Don Dixon & John Bare © 2018

She's the feminist I want to kiss

A Baptist and a Communist

She's got immunity from powers that be

Winks at the sheriff, he pretends he doesn't see

Keeps her bullets with her Bible

Doesn't shave above her knee

Wears a scarf she stole from Newport

And a ring from Galilee

She's a Baptist and a Communist

Shot her man when he raised his fist

She's the feminist I want to kiss

A Baptist and a Communist

A Baptist and a Communist

She's got a happy face but under those bangs

Her mind is always working to facilitate some change

Organizing hotel maids

Marching for a living wage

By the jail she kneels and whispers

Oh, God please calm my rage

She's a Baptist and a Communist

Shot her man when he raised his fist

She's the feminist I want to kiss

A Baptist and a Communist

A Baptist and a Communist

Ohhh, ohhh,

A Baptist and a Communist

The Displaced Man

By Don Dixon & John Bare © 2018

Too old to please the pretty girls, too young to take the needle.

I'm stacking time with Crestor, and a heart that's growing feeble.

A schoolkid took my picture, now it hangs in a museum.

The people stop and shake their heads. I stare back like I see 'em.

Green tea and green label,

keep my mind alert, my liver stable.

Doing less than I am able.

I've become The Displaced Man.

I've become The Displaced Man.

I understand Professor Seagull, and I shook Joe Mitchell's hand.

The girl I loved, I never told her. Now I never can.

I dreamed of San Francisco but wound up in Millbrae.

I used to want a book deal, but now there's nothing left to say.

I've mostly made my peace, don't wonder too much why.

But I still dream of Gimghoul Road, and Pilgrim's Progress makes me cry.

Green tea and green label,

keep my mind alert, my liver stable.

Doing less than I am able.

I've become The Displaced Man.

I've become The Displaced Man.

I've mostly made my peace, don't wonder too much why.

But I still dream of Gimghoul Road, and Pilgrim's Progress makes me cry.

Green tea and green label,

keep my mind alert, my liver stable.

Doing less than I know I am able.

I've become The Displaced Man.

I've become The Displaced Man.

Whiskey Kisses

By Don Dixon & John Bare © 2018

I rubbed a magic lamp

and then I danced around the fire.

Turns out the genie was an angry drunk

whose license had expired.

He yelled at me in Gaelic

and then screwed up all my wishes.

But he left behind this bonnie sprite

who wakes me up with whiskey kisses.

She flies in through the window

and wakes me up with whiskey kisses.

Whiskey kisses.

Even though she spills the Lagavulin.

and she busted up three blenders.

But she bakes fresh pecan sandies.

Well let's forgive this first offender.

Yeah,

Because she wakes me up with whiskey kisses.

Because she wakes me up with whiskey kisses.

She clogs the sink with squoze out limes.

She burns the toast and spills red wine.

She wrecked my car and killed my plants.

She spends my money and lets in ants.

Ohhhh, yeah

But let's forgive this first offender.

Yeah, let's forgive this first offender.

Because she wakes me up with whiskey kisses.

You know she wakes me up with whiskey kisses.

Yeah, she wakes me up with whiskey kisses.

I Fell in Love With Emmylou

By Don Dixon & John Bare © 2018

I became a country DJ
Learned the songs of Willie and Merle
Worshiped at the Church of Hank
Then I heard the Red Dirt Girl
I fell in love with Emmylou
I don't know what to do
Can't tell my wife, but I cannot tell a lie
I fell in love with Emmylou
I became a country DJ
Learned the sounds of Lester and Earl
Found a home in the Church of Hank
Then I heard the Red Dirt Girl
I fell in love with Emmylou
I don't know what to do
Can't tell my wife, but I cannot tell a lie
I fell in love with Emmylou
Grievous angel haunts my sleep
Shows me the devil and the deep blue sea
I fell in love with Emmylou
And now I don't know what to do
(strings)
From the hour of darkest night
I hear her voice on the whippoorwill
She never called me by my name
And I know she never will
Guess things just happen this way
That doesn't dry my tears
Guitar town, and Dublin blues
It's a hard life all these years
I fell in love with Emmylou
I don't know what to do
Can't tell my wife, but I cannot tell a lie
I don't know what to do
I fell in love with Emmylou

Do You Like to Slow Dance?

By Don Dixon & John Bare © 2018

On the Redneck Riviera,

just before ... before the sunrise.

I hook my thumb into your belt loop,

Oh, I'm lost ... I get lost inside your sad eyes.

I feel the earth wobble,

smell the low tide receding.

Your hair damp from tequila,

my sunrise ballerina.

Do you like to slow dance?

Would you like to slow dance?

Do you want to slow dance?

With me?

Do you like to slow dance?

Do you want to slow dance?

Would you like to slow dance?

With me?

Oyster shells for the dance floor.

Nola memories erased.

Your skin seasoned by the salt air.

My brain dizzy ... dizzy from the taste.

Do you like to slow dance?

Would you like to slow dance?

Do you want to slow dance?

With me?

When the planet bobs and weaves,

just before the sun comes up.

Thunder rolls in before true love,

When the biscuits are too damn hot to touch.

Do you like to slow dance?

Would you like to slow dance?

Do you want to slow dance?

With me?

Do you like to slow dance?

Do you want to slow dance?

Would you like to slow dance?

With me?

Brownsville Tonight

By Don Dixon & John Bare © 2018

Buenos noches, mi amigo, have you seen my friend?

Have you seen the pretty girl who taught me how to sin?

Eyes from Matamoros, lips as sweet as whipping cream.

Met her by the old Cortez, down on Jackson Street.

Brillante like the Southern Cross, reflecting Holy light.

You know we're leaving for Havana, on a chartered plane tonight.

How many stars in Boca del Rio? How many stars in old New Orleans?

How many stars in Nuevo Laredo? How many stars in Sweetwater Springs?

How many stars can fit in the sky?

How many stars in Brownsville tonight?

How many stars in Brownsville tonight?

Buenos noches, mi amigo, have you seen my friend?

Have you seen the pretty girl who taught me how to sin?

Empties line the Pearlwood bar, a blind man shoots tequila.

The tourists leave in taxicabs, tweaked out by the dealers.

Mexican topaz, she shimmers in the night.

You know her skin is so electric that it emanates white light.

How many stars in Boca del Rio? How many stars in old New Orleans?

How many stars in Nuevo Laredo? How many stars in Sweetwater Springs?

How many stars can fit in the sky?

How many stars can fit in the sky?

How many stars can fit in the sky?

How many stars in Brownsville tonight?

How many stars in Brownsville tonight?

Redhead from Detroit

By Don Dixon & John Bare © 2018

The redhead from Detroit,

she became a Georgia Peach.

Now she shakes her ass

to an Allman Brothers beat.

She left the Motor City,

where she never did belong.

Now she's in Savannah,

on the right side of the wrong.

The redhead from Detroit.

Redhead, readhead.

The redhead from Detroit.

Now she's hanging out with Southern boys.

She winks at all the silly boys,

full of hope and fear.

She runs on gin and juice

and Sunday morning beer.

She dreams about that big old boat

she knows she'll never own.

She likes to grow Sea Island peas

and she's glad she lives alone.

The redhead from Detroit.

Redhead, readhead.

The redhead from Detroit.

Now she's hanging out with Southern boys.

Her car won't start, tip money's gone.

Weeds in the garden, she's on the right side of the wrong.

At night she works the Dew Drop Inn,

lifting wallets from the rubes.

She's Midnight Rider in spiked heels,

fighting with the moon.

She's a readhead from Detroit,

but she became a Georgia Peach.

Now she shakes her ass

to an Allman Brothers beat.

She left the Motor City,

where she never did belong.

Now she's in Savannah,

on the right side of the wrong.

The redhead from Detroit.

Redhead, readhead.

The redhead from Detroit.

Now she's hanging out with Southern boys.

The redhead from Detroit.

Oh, she's a redhead, readhead.

The redhead from Detroit.

You know she's hanging out with Southern boys.

Whoopee—ooo—ooo

Whooo—hoo hoo

Is Today Monday

By Don Dixon & John Bare © 2018

My calendar's torn, and my mind's feeling worn.

And I've lost all track of time.

Slept on the floor. I shouldn't do that no more.

And I gotta stop doing those lines.

It could be my birthday, more likely my worst day.

I have no idea under the sun.

I got newspapers here, stacked up by the beer.

I need to find the newest one.

Is today Monday, or could it be Sunday.

I really don't know how to find out.

I get drunk and get sober, then do it all over.

The days and the nights are all swirling about.

Is today Sunday, or could it be Monday.

I really don't know how I can tell.

I get drunk and get sober, then do it all over.

It can be heaven, or it can be hell.

My left leg fell asleep, little pains in my feet.

The carpet stuck to my face.

The tape desk is on, cause I DJ'd 'till dawn.

Broken glass all over my place.

One buddy left for L-A. Oh, why did I stay?

I've love to see the left side.

There were broken men here, lots of egos and beer,

Lucky no one died.

Is today Monday, or could it be Sunday.

I really don't know how to find out.

Am I drunk now or sober? Is the week over?

The days and the nights are still jumbled about.

Maybe it's Sunday. But it feels more like Monday.

Where's a newspaper with a date that will tell.

The heartache is coming, and it hurts like hell.

No Songs About Mamas or Trains

By Don Dixon & John Bare © 2018

In her infidelity

She demands

fidelity

She does not cheat on the one she cheated with

She wears a name tag day by day

But on the nights she needs to stray

She wears Dior and buys into the myth

She buys into the myth

Sets the rules for the game

No kissing her lips

No songs about mamas or trains

. . . songs about mamas or trains

No songs about mamas or trains

No sermons from pilgrims, no Hank Williams refrains

Give her Etta and Elmore and everything James

But no songs about mamas or trains.

She stays out on the town

Til the pain lets go and drowns

in the sounds of 2120

or anything but Townes

anything but Townes

For hanging in her closet

With Pueblo Waltz running through the weave

Is the barroom dress, frayed and grayed

She wears pouring those shots and carryin those sevens on her sleeves

But tonight Loretta is dancing with the myth

Locked in a lonely game

No touching her lips

No songs about mamas or trains

So no songs about mamas or trains

No sermons from pilgrims, no Hank Williams refrains

Give her Chess, and give her the Staxx and all those Motown names

But no songs about mamas or trains.

. . . mamas or trains

Bougainvillea Blues

By Don Dixon & John Bare © 2018

Why buy when you can rent? Why rent when you can steal?
Don't bother me with interest rates. Just show me my next meal.
Out here on the vineyard, with my patent leather shoes
Turn the TV off. I've got the Bougainvillea Blues.
And gas lines are for suckers. Credit lines are crimes.
Mermaids have no hemlines, and I take my bath in wine.
Out here on the vineyard, there's no way I can lose.
The mailman don't deliver. I've got the Bougainvillea Blues.
Four quarters make a dollar. Ten dollars make a day.
Grilled cheese is a liar's meal, and Dylan sings okay.
Whooo . . .
Oh, out here on the vineyard, we dance to Peggy Sue.
I can't find my keys. I've got the Bougainvillea Blues.
Don't drive to Nova Scotia. Teach me some semaphore.
Always pass the butter. And never slam the door.
Out here on the vineyard, the hummingbird make rules.
Jack and Jill fell down the hill, I've got the Bougainvillea Blues.
We surfed with Linda Ronstadt. I cooked for Raquel Welch.
Those tattoos never turn out right, and memories just melt.
Out here on the vineyard, with my patent leather shoes
Turn on the radio. I've got the Bougainvillea Blues.
Out here on the vineyard, with my patent leather shoes
Turn on the radio. I've got the Bougainvillea Blues.
I've got the Bougainvillea Blues.
I've got the Bougainvillea Blues.

About the Author

John Bare is a photographer, songwriter, and former journalist who has worked for more than two decades in the nonprofit sector. With Don Dixon, John wrote songs for the 2019 album, *Lassie James Songbook Vol. I*, a collection of twelve original songs inspired by this novel. John was born in Winston-Salem and attended public schools in Garner, NC, where his parents were educators. He attended the University of North Carolina, where he studied film as an undergraduate, received a PhD in mass communication research, and developed an appreciation for biscuits, whiskey, and live music. John shares his house with rescue dogs Winston and Isadora.